"A dark heart-stopper."

—*Boston Herald*

"For years, those of us in the know have read Ken Bruen. Now the rest of the world is catching on."

—Mark Billingham, author of *Sleepyhead*

"A soul mate of Jim Thompson's, or maybe James M. Cain's."

—*The Irish Times*

"A brisk, punchy read that's defiantly fresh and original, and more emotionally true than the majority of books. Irishman Bruen is one helluva a writer."

—*January Magazine*

"You've never read a book quite like this one. Bruen writes in a sleek, creative, and distinct style. He also knows how to produce a knockout ending you might not see coming."

—*Rocky Mountain News*

"A strong piece of crime writing."

—*Booklist*

"Bruen's hard-boiled style is perfect for his tale. What makes *The Killing of the Tinkers* a four-star delight is Bruen's deft narrative skills."

—*Boston Globe*

"A Celtic Dashiell Hammett."

—*The Philadelphia Inquirer*

"A stellar crime novel."

—*Toronto Globe and Mail*

"Gloriously entertaining. Bruen's twisted genius lies in blending noir elements with humor. What's next for Jack? Hard to say. Whatever happens, you get the feeling Bruen will delight us with his darkness all over again."

—*Miami Herald*

"A dazzling piece of work. Bruen's style is clipped, caustic, heartbreaking, and often hilarious."

—*Cleveland Plain Dealer*

Praise for Ken Bruen for *The Guards*

"Bruen is a brilliant, lyrical, deeply moving writer who can make you laugh and cry in the same paragraph and whose characters are so sharply portrayed that they almost walk off the page at you. If you like Ian Rankin, Dennis Lehane, George Pelecanos, and the like, Bruen is definitely a writer to reckon with."

—*Denver Post*

"The next major new Irish voice we hear might well belong to Ken Bruen."

—*Chicago Tribune*

"Bruen is an original, grimly hilarious and gloriously Irish. I await the further adventures of the incorrigible Jack Taylor."

—Patrick Anderson, *The Washington Post*

"Bruen's astringent prose and death's-head humor keep this quest for redemption from getting maudlin, just as his 'tapestry of talk' makes somber poetry of the barstool laments that serve as dialogue. Even in barrooms, 'there are poets among us,' and sometimes their voices are fierce."

—Marilyn Stasio, *The New York Times Book Review*

"The story is dark and the style is elegant, smooth, spare, and silky as the best aged Irish whiskey. Sharp, swift, and blackly comic."

—*Portsmouth Herald*

"Bracing, eccentric, hard-boiled, unforgettable."

—*New Orleans Times-Picayune*

"[Ken Bruen's] clipped, bleak writing style captures the pervasive brooding Irish landscape better than any author in a very long while."

—*BookPage*

"Hard-boiled, eccentric, darkly comic: Bruen bows to but doesn't just mimic James M. Cain and the other great noirists in a breakout novel not to be missed."

—*Kirkus Reviews* (starred review)

"Outstanding. Bruen has a rich and mordant writing style, full of offbeat humor. Perhaps the standard bearer for a new subgenre called 'Hibernian Noir.' "

—*Publishers Weekly* (starred review)

"Ken Bruen is a wonder, and has developed a dazzling style of story-telling—call it White Hot Irish Blues—that sizzles on the page. His novels are gritty, funny, terse, and very, very dark—but also surprisingly compassionate. By far, the coolest books I've read this year."

—C. J. Box, author of *Winterkill* and *Trophy Hunt*

"*The Guards* blew me away. It's dark, funny, and moving—just for starters. With a sharp eye and a lyrical voice, Ken Bruen takes us on a powerful odyssey through the mean streets of Galway, straight into the Irish heart. Bruen's tale is a potent draft of desire and hopelessness, conviction and surrender, inadvertent heroism and unexpected grace. This is mystery writing of a high order."

—T. Jefferson Parker, author of *Black Water* and *Silent Joe*

"*The Guards* is a wonderful book, wrenching and real, fast, funny, and wise in every sense. Why the hell haven't I heard of Ken Bruen before? He's a terrific writer and *The Guards* is one of the most mesmerizing works of crime fiction I've ever read. I'm going to read the rest of his work now, so don't bother me for a while. And when he's got a new one, send it to me quick. This guy is the real thing."

—James W. Hall, author of *Blackwater Sound*

"*The Guards* is raw, hard, bitter, and amazing. It's got that ancient feel to it, as of a primal story being retold with a fine, careless Irish swagger. It's as if Bruen made up his mind to tell us this story whether we wanted to hear it or not. Oh we do. For sure."

—Jon A. Jackson, author of *Badger Games*

"*The Guards* is an astounding novel, a poetic account of a desperation as deep and cold as the North Sea, retribution, and resurrection. It's so good I can't think of it as a crime novel. It's a fine book with some crimes."

—James Crumley, author of *The Final Country*

"*The Guards* kicked my ass, it's up there with the best. If Elmore Leonard got together with James Joyce to write a Spenser novel, this is what you'd get!"

—David Means, author of *Assorted Fire Events*

Praise for *The Killing of the Tinkers*

"Bruen confirms his rightful place among the finest noir stylists of his generation. This is a remarkable book from a singular talent."

—*Publishers Weekly* (starred review)

Ken Bruen

The Killing of the Tinkers

ST. MARTIN'S MINOTAUR NEW YORK

www.minotaurbooks.com

Library of Congress Cataloging-in-Publication Data

Bruen, Ken.
    The killing of the tinkers / Ken Bruen.
        p. cm.
    ISBN 0-312-30411-0 (hc)
    ISBN 0-312-33928-3 (pbk)
    EAN 978-0312-33928-9
    1. Private investigators—Ireland—Galway—Fiction. 2. Ex-police officers—Fiction. 3. Galway (Ireland)—Fiction. I. Title

PR6052.R785K55 2004
823'.914—dc22   2003058559

First published in Ireland by Brandon, and imprint of Mount Eagle Publications

First St. Martin's Griffin Edition: March 2005

10 9 8 7 6 5 4 3 2 1

For Ed McBain
and
Bonnie and Joe,
Black Orchid Bookshop,
East 81st St., New York

You Can't Go Home Again

Thomas Wolfe

The boy is back in town. As the coach pulled into Galway, Thin Lizzie was loud in my head. One of the great solo blasts from Gary Moore. I saw them at their last gig in Dublin. I had pulled crowd duty for the biggest concert of the year. Phil Lynott, head to toe in black leather, coked to the gills. He stalked that stage like Rilke's panther. He'd never stalk a stage again. Me neither. His premature death coincided with my own career crash. I'd been booted out of the guards for slapping a TD in the mouth. I'd never regretted that. Only wish I'd hit him harder. My dismissal led into a spiral of slow descent towards alcoholic hell. Settling in Galway, I'd become a half-assed private investigator, causing more havoc than the crimes I'd been investigating. Now I was bringing back from London a leather coat and a coke habit.

I would have come home sooner, but for the old Irish imperative of having to stay gone. At least look like you tried.

I don't know whom I was trying to impress. It had been a long time since I'd impressed a living soul, least of all myself. A near miracle had happened. My departure from Galway had been a sober one. It was such a revelation. To be clear in my mind and free from the habitual sickness was amazing. I could think without the need to swill booze at every opportunity. Reading books returned to being the pleasure it had once been. I truly believed I was about to start anew.

Now I was back to being what they call a conscious drinker. When I was conscious, I was drinking. A fellah I met on the Kilburn High Road had asked me if I was a social drinker. I'd said,

"No, what about yourself?"

"I'm a social security drinker."

I'd gone to London with a plan. There are few things more lethal than an alcoholic with a plan. Here was mine. Go to London and get a flat in Bayswater. As near to the park as it gets. Preferably with a bay window. Watch those grey squirrels along the Serpentine. In the plan, the woman I'd loved would come to her senses and realise how much she missed me. She'd fly to London and, somehow or other, she'd find me. Just one fine day, it would have to be a fine day, she'd miraculously find me, and happiness would be sealed. All I had to do was wait and she'd show. Or if I stayed away long enough, a letter would arrive from her, telling me how much she missed me and would I please take her back?

What I got was a bedsitter in Ladbroke Grove. Consoled

myself with delusion. I'd been weaned on Van Morrison's "Astral Weeks". Among a richness of great songs, "Astral Weeks" stood out. Told myself I was living it. The reality was as close to nightmare as you get. The grove is now a long stretch of urban decay. The human wreckage vies for space with the garbage. A mix of aromas hits you as soon as you begin to venture along it. From the inevitable curry through urine to that pervasive stench of abandonment.

Leaving Galway, I'd left behind a string of deaths. My case had involved the apparent suicide of a teenage girl. The investigation had led to—

Witness this:

Three murders.

Four, if you count my best friend.

My heart being hammered.

Tons of cash.

Exile.

Imagine if I'd been competent.

Oh yeah, and there's the possibility that my involvement caused the death of a teenage girl. I had to bite down and swallow hard lest I add my own name to the list of fatalities. I could trot out the sickest defence line of the decade:

"I meant well."

I didn't.

I was too drunk most of the time to mean anything.

As the coach approached the outskirts of the city, I'd mouthed a mantra:

"Attempting to give back to the world a portion of its lost heart."

The quotation by Louise Brogan, it gave me a sense of longing I couldn't ever expect to realise.

Getting off the coach at Fair Green, the first thing I saw was the headline:

MORE GARDAÍ FOR GALWAY'S VIOLENT STREETS

Next I noticed the hotels. Four more in Forster Street. This used to be the arse end of town. Nothing grew here ever. Of course, Sammon's was long gone. The pub of my youth. Liam Sammon had played on the team that won three All Irelands.

Count them and weep. At least when the pub went, we'd still had the carpet showroom A sign in the window said "Moved to the Tuam Road".

Jesus.

You could no longer say,

"Everything's gone to hell."

Hell and everything else had moved to the Tuam Road.

Before my departure, I'd found a new pub. No mean achievement in a city that had barred me from every worthwhile establishment. I knew it was my kind of pub from the sign in the window.

WE DO NOT STOCK BUD LIGHT.

Jeff, the owner, had been part of a heavy metal band. Big in
the eighties, in Germany. He wrote the lyrics. You go . . . what
lyrics?

Exactly.

He'd hooked up with a punk rocker who odd times helped
me. Cathy Bellingham, a Londoner ex-junkie, she'd washed up
in Galway. I'd introduced them and withdrawn. They'd be my
first port of call.

I'd flown from Heathrow to Dublin, caught the noon coach
west. The driver said,

"Howyah?"

I knew I was home.

A reformed smoker, I'd started again. It's a bastard. The new
world is designed for non-smokers. It's near impossible to do
coke and not smoke. It blends so fine. When that first rush hits,
you want to wallop it with nicotine. As if you're not bad
enough. I don't know is it when that ice numbness jells or
later, but you're reaching for that soft red pack. Try smoking at
Dublin Airport or any airport. Good luck. Talk about segrega-
tion. Small pockets of isolation where the shamed smokers
congregate. Like lepers of the modern wasteland. You'd nod
guiltily at each other, crank the lighter and suck the poison in.
You'd need your head examined to bring drugs through
Dublin Airport. These guys are lethal. Boy, do they see you
coming. Get you and you are going down.

I chanced it.

My need was greater than my fear. I could envision the headline:

EX–GARDA BUSTED AT AIRPORT

Wouldn't that launch a homecoming?

Phew-oh.

On Forster Street the urge to snort was massive, but I held it off. Outside Nestor's a guy in a filthy white suit was singing,

"You're such a good-looking woman."

A battered cap was at his feet. It had collected all of 50p. I checked my pockets, put a few coins down. He said,

"Spit on me, Dickie."

From Joe Dolan to Dickie Rock, without missing a beat. I laughed and he added,

"That's sterling."

"Sorry."

"Ary, you meant well."

He launched into "The House with the Whitewashed Gable".

A lone sentry at the bar. He exclaimed,

"Jaysus, look who's back."

Irish people across the board will greet a returnee with exactly the same expression,

"You're back."

Jeff was behind the bar, nodded, asked,

"What'll it be?"

"A pint."

The question was large in his eyes:

"You're drinking again?"

Fair fuck to him, he didn't ask it. A song was playing, something I didn't recognise. I asked,

"What's the tune?"

He smiled, said,

"You're not going to believe this."

"Jeff, it's Ireland; I'll believe anything."

"It's 'I Saw a Stranger' by Tommy Fleming."

Leaving the Guinness to settle, he came round and said,

"Gimme a hug."

I did.

Not easily or with much flexibility. Us Irish guys don't do hugs. Not without a lingering mortification. He looked good. His trademark black 501s were spotless. A granddad shirt, cowboy boots and a black suede waistcoat. A ponytail tied tight. Like me, Jeff was knocking on fifty. He didn't look like an aging rocker. An ease in his movements gave class to whatever he wore. I said,

"You look great."

In Ireland this is usually the preamble to "Lend us some money."

I meant it.

He stepped back, scrutinised me. I was wearing my one Oxfam suit. It had died. I'd let my hair grow and hadn't trimmed my beard. He said,

"You look fucked."

"Thanks."

He went to cream the pint. I sat at what used to be my spot. In the corner, hard chair, harder table. Hadn't changed. I had. I said to the sentry,

"Can I get you a pint?"

He didn't answer for a moment. I wasn't sure he'd heard. Then he spun on the stool, asked,

"Will I have to buy you one back?"

"No."

"OK then."

I rummaged in my holdall, took out some essentials. Left a package on the table, slipped the rest in my pocket, said,

"Jeff, I'm just going for a pee."

"Whatever."

I locked a stall, kneeled over the toilet, pulled down the lid, took out the Silverwrap. I laid five lines, rolled an English tenner and snorted fast. The burn was instant. Rocked me against the door, could feel the freeze lash my brain, muttered,

"Christ."

After ten minutes, I was electric; straightened up, went to the wash basin. A mirror above had the logo,

SWEET AFTON.

My nose was bleeding. I said,

"Sweet Jesus."

Cleansed it with a tissue. Doused my face in cold water. A grey tint showed beneath my beard. My cheeks were sunken. I hitched my pants, tightened the belt a notch. Two stone had gone. In my hurling days, I was built. Spuds and sport pack on that bulk.

Back in the bar, Cathy was sitting at my table. Transformed. I'd known a twenty-two-year-old punk with track marks on her arms. She jumped up, said,

"You're back."

Alongside the Irish greeting, she'd acquired a soft lilt. I preferred her Kim Carnes intonation.

More hugging.

She gave me the look, said,

"Coke."

"Hey."

"You can't fool an old doper."

"Why would I try?"

"Because it's what addicts do . . . hide."

I sat, took a hefty swig of my drink. God, it was good. Cathy leant over, wiped the foam of my upper lip, said,

"We have your room ready."

"What?"

"Your first night, you have to be with friends."

"I was going back to Bailey's."

"Go tomorrow."

"Well, OK."

She'd filled out. Her face was well-fed, shining even. I said,

"You look radiant."

She went shy; I'd swear she blushed, though I think that's a lost art. She said,

"I'm pregnant."

After I did the congratulations bit, I said,

"I bought ye something."

Her face lit, she asked,

"Show me."

I gave her the first package. Like a child, she tore it open. A gold Claddagh ring bounced on the table. I said,

"I got ye both one."

"Oh, Jack."

I'd got them off a guy in a pub.

Cathy tried the ring. It fit. She called,

"Hon, come see what Jack bought?"

He approached the table cautiously. Cathy showed him the gold ring, said,

"Go on, try it."

Didn't fit so hot. He pulled a chain from beneath his shirt. I spotted a miraculous medal. He opened the clasp, slid the ring along the links, said,

"Daniel Day-Lewis wears one, figures it makes him Irish."

The medal sat on the table, like an aspiration, leastways the coke thought so. Jeff said,

"Jack, you take it."

"It probably belonged to your mother."

"She'd appreciate a worthy cause."

"Put like that, how can I refuse?"

I put it in my wallet. There was a photograph, showed a young woman smiling at something off camera. Her hair in ringlets, framing a face of neat prettiness. Jeff caught a glimpse, said,

"Oh, yeah?"

"Came with the wallet."

The night turned into a party. I rang Mrs Bailey at my old hotel and she arrived with Janet, the maid/chamberperson/pot walloper. A true creature of grace. A few guards showed and joined in. By nine, the place was hopping. I'd switched to Bush and the going was easy. Jeff danced with Mrs Bailey, I had a waltz with Janet. The guards did some jigs.

Post party. The pub looked like a bomb had hit it. I'd passed out on my hard chair. Bad idea. My back was in bits. The hangover hit low, fast and lethal, walloping every fibre of my being. I muttered,

"Sweet mother of Jesus."

The sentry had crashed on the bar, the inevitable half pint of black at his head. Jeff appeared, greeted,

"Nice morning for it, lads."

Sadistic bastard. He turned on the TV. Surfing the channels, he settled on Sky News, heard,

"Paula Yates has been found dead."

Hit me like thunder. I loved that lost chick. Once heard her say,

"The first time Fifi fell off the bed as a baby, I raced to the doctor. I was beside myself. He said the only thing wrong with this baby is she is wearing too much jewellery."

How could you not love her?

A time I heard Mary Coughlan say,

"It's one thing to sing the blues; feeling them nearly killed me."

Amen.

Jeff shook his head, stared at me, said,

"What a waste."

But I knew. His expression was beloved of mothers, length and breadth of the country. It cautioned,

"Let that be a lesson to you."

Jeff had way too much style to say that. The sentry stirred, reached for his glass, drained the dregs, then went back to sleep. In my old pub, Grogan's, two men were in constant attendance. Each end of the bar, dressed identically

Cloth caps

Donkey jackets

Terylene pants.

Twin drinks. Always and for ever, the half drained pint of Guinness, creamy head intact. No mean achievement. I'd never known them acknowledge each other. I knew them as the sentries only. What they were guarding is anybody's guess. The old values perhaps. One had fallen to a coronary. The second had shifted his tent when Grogan's changed hands.

I felt old. Circling fifty, every bad year was etched on my face. The hangover threw in another hard five. Jeff asked,

"Coffee?"

"Does the pope have beads?"

"That's a yes?"

I headed upstairs. They'd given me the attic room. It was clean, Spartan. Thomas Merton could have swung a cat in it. Sunlight streamed in through the roof window. It gave me an illusion of hope. Got my toilet gear and went in search of a bathroom. It was unoccupied. Spotlessly maintained, with a crescendo of fluffy towels. I said,

"O . . . K."

Tore off my ruined suit and got into the shower. As best I could, I avoided seeing my torso. Numerous beatings had left a sorry legacy. Turned the tap to scalding and let the bastard roar. Eased out with my skin tingling. Wrapped in one of those towels, I checked their cabinet.

Doesn't everybody?

Lots of female stuff. Sprayed on a Mum deodorant. The fumes nearly choked me. Shook loose some family aspirin and dry swallowed them. There was a bottle of aftershave in a striking metal flask. Named Harley. I thought,

"C'mon, Jeff."

Massaged it into my beard, said,

"Things go better with coke."

Set up some lines on the sink, took a deep breath and snorted. A few moments, nothing doing. Thought maybe the hangover was riding shotgun. Then angels sang. The rush was related to nausea. Could feel my eyes open wide. Man, I wasn't hurting no more. Skipped back to my room, muttering,

"I love my life."

Selected a faded pair of Levi cords. One more wash and

they were history. A sweatshirt with the logo "Filthy McNasty's". Courtesy of Shane McGowan's local in Islington. It had been white, but I washed it alongside a navy shirt. Finally a pair of shoes. Shook free a Marlboro, lit up. Me and Bette Davis, still smoking. Headed down to the bar, grabbed a mouthful of coffee. Perfect, bitter as a rumour. Jeff said,

"Must be some powerful eye drops."

"What?"

"Your eyes . . . they're glowing."

Cathy appeared, said,

"Phew, I am like, never, ever going to drink Spritzers again."

Jeff told her about Paula Yates. She said,

"Poor bitch."

A little later, leaning close to me, she asked,

"What's that scent? You smell like my Jeff."

Her effortless embrace of his name tore at my heart.

I moved to my chair, let out a deep breath. I was well on the way to recovery. The door opened and a heavyset man entered. He had a full black beard, an expression of quiet energy. He approached, asked,

"Might I have a word?"

"Sure."

"A quiet word."

I looked round the pub, not a haven of privacy. I got my smile in gear, said,

"Let's step outside."

A tiny pull at the corner of his mouth, the only indication he appreciated the joke. One glance at his hands, you knew he'd travelled the route. The fresh air hit me like a hurley. I staggered, felt a steadying hand. He said,

"Fresh air can be a whore."

I pulled out my smokes, shook one free, cranked the lighter. Nothing doing. I said,

"Fuck."

He was wearing a dark suit, white shirt, knotted tie. He reached inside his jacket, produced a Zippo, handed it over. It was solid silver. I fired up, offered it back. He said,

"Hang on to it; I quit."

"It's solid silver."

"Let's call it a loan."

"OK."

I sat on the window ledge, asked,

"What's on your mind?"

"You know me?"

"Nope."

"You're sure?"

"I don't forget faces."

"I'm Sweeper."

I checked his face. He wasn't kidding.

"No offence, pal, but it doesn't mean shit to me."

"The tinkers?"

"Is this some kind of joke?"

"I'm a man of little humour, Mr Taylor."

"Call me Jack. So . . . what do you want?"

"Help."

"I don't know how I could do that."

"You helped Ann Henderson."

Her name caught me blindside, like a screech across my soul.
Must have shown in my face. He said,

"I regret causing you sorrow, Mr Taylor."

"Jack, it's Jack."

I flicked the cigarette, watched it arch high, then fall. I said,

"Look, Sweep . . . Jesus . . . what a name. I don't do that any
more."

"She said you'd help."

"She was wrong."

I began to move. He put out his hands, said,

"They're killing our people."

It's a show-stopper. No question. It stopped me. Turned to
face him. He said,

"You've been away. I know that. In the past six months, four
travellers have been killed."

He paused, contempt in his eyes, continued,

"The guards, they've done nothing. I went to the superintendent, a man named Clancy. Do you know of him?"

I nodded and he said,

"For them, it's only tinkers . . . and everybody knows,
they're always killing each other."

"What do you think I can do?"

"You can find out."

"Find out what?"

"Who's killing them and why."

Children of the Dead End

Patrick McGill

I ended up staying in Nestor's for a few more days. Mainly because I couldn't get it together to move. It was round noon, I was levelling out. Shouted Jeff for a pint. He asked,

"Bit early for it?"

"Jeez, I'm up since eight."

He glanced at my eyes, said,

"You're up all right."

I was sliding on a downer, snapped,

"Forget it."

Jeff doesn't do retaliation, began to pour a pint, said,

"What's your hurry?"

I eased, said,

"Time I checked into Bailey's."

"Take a few more days. Cathy is glad of the company."

I watched him cream the pint before I ventured,

"And you, Jeff, what's your take?"

"I'm your friend, I don't have a take."

Is there a reply to this? I don't know it. The door opened and Sweeper came in. A blue suit and a bluer shirt, wool tie. Except for a gold earring, he could have passed for a guard. The temptation to pun was ferocious.

Like,

"Look what the car swept in."

Instead I said,

"Join me."

"A mineral, please."

Jeff checked.

"Club Orange?"

"Yes, please."

We studied each other for a moment, then Sweeper took a swallow of the drink. Crunched the ice, revealing strong white teeth. I said,

"What's on your mind?"

"You are in need of digs?"

"No . . . no, I'm not. I'm up to my eyes in accommodation."

He gave the brief smile, said,

"You have the sharp tongue."

"I like to cut to the chase."

He produced a set of keys, placed them on the table, said,

"You'll know Hidden Valley."

"Of course . . . John Arden lives there."

"Who?"

"Booker Prize nominee, highly respected dramatist . . ."

He put up his hand,

"I'm not a bookish man, Mr Taylor."

"Never too late."

"I didn't say I'm unlearnt . . . I said something else entirely."

Saw the flash in his eyes. Cautioned myself not to fuck with him.

Fucked with him anyway, said,

"Hit a nerve, did I?"

He ignored that, said,

"Some of my people bought a house there. They . . . didn't settle. I'd like to offer you the house. It's small but adequate."

"And you'll give me this if I help."

"Yes."

"What if I don't find anything?"

"The house is yours for six months."

My instincts said,

"No."

I said,

"You've got a deal."

Picked up the keys, said,

"Tell me what happened."

He produced a scrap of paper, laid it down. I looked at it.

Jan. 3rd ....Christy Flynn (Óg)
Feb. 19th ....Cionn Flaherty
April 2nd...Seaneen Brown
June 9th...Blackie Ryan

I asked,

"All dead?"

"Aye, found in the Fair Green, near the Simon House."

"How?"

"How what?"

"Did they die?"

"Their heads crushed with a hammer."

He got up abruptly, went to the bar, asked Jeff,

"A small Jameson and a pint for my friend."

I looked at the list. A weariness came whispering at my soul:

"You are so tired."

A line I'd once heard came to mind:

"He drank, not because of the darkness in him but the darkness in others."

Sweeper returned, asked,

"Payment?"

"What?"

"How much cash do you want?"

"Aren't you giving me a bloody house?"

"You'll need money, everybody does."

Argue that.

He'd given me a fat envelope, stuffed with notes. I said,

"Wish it had been brown."

He was lost, said,

"I'm lost."

"A brown envelope, we could have been TDs."

The quip was not to his taste. He sipped at the Jameson like a man who's been badly burnt. Whiskey had scorched me more times than I want to recall. A look between us and he said,

"I have to ration it."

"Hey, I'm the last guy who needs an explanation."

"I know."

"Excuse me?"

"Ann Henderson told me of your affliction."

Rage burned. I asked,

"Affliction . . . she said that?"

He waved his left hand, vague in his dismissal.

"My people suffer similarly."

I let it go . . . fuck it.

Time to pack. I said,

"Give me a few minutes and I'll be ready."

Upstairs, I packed my holdall, nicked the bottle of Harley. Jeff smelled fine. I, however, needed all the assistance available. Put on my London leather. Creaked a bit, but I could call that character. Down to the bar, put out my hand to Jeff, said,

"It's been fun."

"Where are you going?"

The sentry raised his head, shouted,

"He's going with the tinker."

Jeff clipped him, said,

"Hey."

Sweeper nodded, went outside. I said,

"I've got a house in Hidden Valley."

"From yer man?"

"Yes."

"What's the catch?"

"I'm going to look into a bit of trouble he's had."

"Jeez, Jack, I thought you packed in that business . . . after last time."

"This is different."

"Yea, you're in even worse shape. Cathy! Jack is going."

She came running.

"Aw, Jack."

"I'll be near, literally round the corner."

"But I had a fillum."

She pronounced it thus. When the English go native, they go bananas.

"What film?"

"*Julien Donkey-Boy* by Harmony Korine."

I gave her my best blank look. She continued,

"It's the Dogme #6 one. He made *Gummo*, remember?"

"Um, not offhand."

"Jack, you have to see it. He takes the piss with Lars von Trier."

Jeff was pissing himself behind the counter. Even the sentry was smiling. I decided to come clean, said,

"None of that makes the slightest sense to me."

Crestfallen, she produced a small package. I could see "Zhivago Records" on the front. She said,

"This was to welcome you home."

I opened the package, a CD titled "You Win Again" by Van

Morrison and Linda Lewis. I mustered all my enthusiasm, muttered,

"Wow."

Cheered now, she gushed,

"I knew you'd be happy. Remember before you went away, you gave me her album."

I didn't, said,

"Sure."

Outside, Sweeper said,

"I've a van."

"Me, too."

It was a Ford Transit, beaten to a pulp. When he saw my reluctance, he said,

"The engine is hyped."

Slid the door and threw my bag in. The white suited singer from my homecoming approached, asked,

"Price of a cup of tea, sir?"

Handed him the CD. He asked,

"What the fuck is this?"

"New material."

I was arrested my first night in Hidden Valley. They came for me at eight, rousing me from a power nap. I'd fallen asleep by an open fire. Hidden Valley is a steep incline running from Prospect Hill to the Headford Road. A haven of rare quiet in a city gone ape. From the hill, you can see out over Lough Corrib, wish for children you never had. To the north is Bohermore. Round the corner is Woodquay and Roches Stores. The house was a modern two up, two down. And hallelujah, wood floors, stone fireplace. Fully furnished with heavy Swedish chairs and sofa. Even the bookcase was full. Sweeper said,

"The fridges and deep freeze are stocked. There's drink in the cupboard."

"You were expecting me?"

"Mr Taylor, we're always expecting someone."

"What can I say? Let me get you a drink?"

"No, I must be away."

I'd once come across a letter written by Williams Burroughs to Allen Ginsberg.

I was first arrested when I beached, a balsa raft suspected to have floated up from Peru with a young boy and a toothbrush. (I travel light, only the essentials.) One night, after shooting six ampoules of dolophine, the ex-captain found me sitting stark naked in the hall on the toilet seat (which I had wrenched from its mooring) playing in a bucket of water and singing "Deep in the Heart of Texas".

I looked round my new home and thought, I've beached pretty well. I had a long bath, put my clothes away and rummaged about. The coal bunker was out back, and I got a fire going. Intended to sit for a few minutes, drifted off. Banging on the door pulled me awake. Wiping sleep from my eyes, I fumbled to the door, opened it and said,

"The guards."

In uniform. Looking about sixteen. But mean with it. The first said,

"Jack Taylor?"

"As if you didn't know."

The second said,

"We'd like you to come with us."

"Why?"

The first smiled, said,

"To help us with our enquiries."

"Can I grab some coffee?"

"I'm afraid not."

The squad car was parked right by the door. I said,

"Thanks for the discretion, lads. I wanted to impress the neighbours."

Just like the movies, the guard put his hand on my head as he put me into the back. Almost looks like care, managed to bang my head, went,

"Oops."

At Mill Street, as we got out, Mike Shocks, the local photographer, rushed over, asked,

"Anybody?"

"Naw, he's nobody."

Inside, I was brought to the interview room. Rubbed my wrists as if I'd been cuffed. A tin ashtray sat centre on a graffiti surface: a logo, "Players Please". I shook loose a red, cranked the Zippo. Deep drag and tried to guess where the camera was. Door opened and Clancy entered. Superintendent Clancy. Man, we had history, none of it good. He'd been present at the action that cost me my career. Then, he'd been skinny as a wet greyhound. We'd been friends. During the events before my exile, he'd been a bastard.

Dressed in the full regalia, he'd leaped into middle age. His face was purple, blotches on the cheeks. The eyes, though, sharp as ever. He said,

"You're back."

"Well detected."

"I'd hoped we'd seen the last of you."

"What can I tell you, bro?"

"I only hope that other yoke, Sutton, won't show up."

"I doubt it."

Sutton was dead. I'd killed him, my best friend. With, as they say, malice afterthought. Clancy walked behind me. The old ritual of intimidation. Rule one of interrogation. Not in the training manual but laid in stone. I said,

"Fair cop, guv; I'll spill my guts."

Sensed his hand raised, tensed as I waited for the wallop. It didn't come. I shook another red loose, fired it up. He asked,

"What are you doing with the tinkers?"

"Tinker."

"Don't give me cheek. I'll run your arse up to Mountjoy before you can scream barrister."

"Oh, you mean Sweeper."

Rage exploded from him. He went,

"He's a blackguard."

"I don't think he's fond of you either."

He plonked himself on the edge of the table, his pants riding up. A white hairless leg was visible above his navy sock. He leaned right into my face. His breath stank of onions. He said,

"Listen to me, laddie. Stay away from that bunch."

I ground out the cigarette, asked,

"You won't be investigating the murders of four of their men?"

Spittle lit the corners of his mouth. He spat,

"Fecking tinkers, they're always killing each other."

He stood up, adjusted the tight tunic, said,

"Get out."

"I'm free to go?"

"Watch your step, boyo."

On my way to the door, I said,

"God bless."

On release from Mill Street, I walked towards Shop Street.
Radiohead's Thom Yorke said,

Every day you think, well maybe, we should stop. Maybe there's
no point to this, because all the sounds you made, that made you
happy, have been sucked of everything they meant. It's a total
headfuck.

I stood on the bridge for a few moments. Across the water,
over near Claddagh, I could see Nimmo's Pier. Sutton's body
had never been found. His paintings were now collectable.
The French have a word for nightmare . . . *cauchemar.* Man,
that is evocative. An alcoholic has dreams to rival that of any
Vietnam vet. Closing your eyes you mutter, "Incoming" . . .
and kidding you ain't. Initially, like the worst irony, alcohol
dispels them. Leastways you don't remember. Then, of course,
it fuels and powder-kegs them to the ninth level. Not a level

on which to linger. The Irish for dreams is *broinglóidí*, a beautiful gentle sound. Of the many impossibles, a drinker prays most in that direction. In vain. I never dream of Sutton. Sure, I think about him most days, but he remains in the daylight hours. Thank Christ.

I needed Merton and a pint. Not necessarily in that order. Headed for Charlie Byrne's, a second-hand bookshop. It is *the* bookshop. During my apprenticeship with the librarian Tommy Kennedy, as he shaped and nurtured my reading, he told me about Sylvia Beach. In Paris, in the true glory days, her bookshop held court to

> Joyce
> Hemingway
> Fitzgerald
> Gertrude Stein
> Ford Maddox Ford

Mr Kennedy's voice would get such a sound of longing in the telling. As he recounted the near mythic atmosphere, I could smell the Gauloise, the aroma of pure French coffee. Being young, naturally, I asked,

"Did you go there, Mr Kennedy?"

With such loss in his eyes, he said,

"No, no . . . I didn't."

One of my embracing poems is *Howl* by Ginsberg. Nobody I ever told ever seemed surprised. I guess they'd heard me howl too often. It travelled back from London in the pocket of my jacket. The other travel book was *The Hound of Heaven*. It had been a collectors' item, bound in calf with gold trim. When I told Tommy Kennedy of my career choice—the guards—he'd been bitterly disappointed. My farewell present from him was the Thompson book. Nights of drunkenness had marred that beautiful volume.

Charlie Byrne's comes close to Tommy's ideal. Some years before, I'd been lurking in the crime section. A student had a beautiful American edition of Walt Whitman. He was peering at the price. Charlie, passing, said,

"Take it with you."

"I haven't enough."

"Ary, settle it some other time."

AND

Handed him *The Collected Robert Frost*, adding,

"You'll want this, too."

Class.

Vinny Brown was surfing the net, looked up, said,

"You're back."

The hardcore team: Charlie, Vinny and Anthony. I'd introduced Anthony to Pellicanos, and in return he'd given me the complete Harry Crews. An American, he seems to understand the pace of Galway. I still don't. Vinny asked,

"How was London?"

I'd recently ploughed through *London: The Biography* by Peter Ackroyd. Trying not to sound too smart-ass, I said,

"London is chaos, an unknowable labyrinth."

Took Vinny a time, then he ventured,

"Ackroyd?"

I don't know about serendipity. I don't mean Sting's atrocious song but coincidence. When God is playing a lower profile. There was a travelling woman in the children's section. Weighing the difference between Barney and *The Velveteen Rabbit*. I nodded and she said,

"Mr Taylor?"

That "Mr" is a killer. I asked,

"You doing OK?"

"There's the replay on Sunday."

"There is?"

"I said a prayer we'd beat the Kingdom. Do you think that's all right?"

"Against Kerry, I'll go and light a candle myself."

She gave me the full look. It's no relation to inquisitiveness, but it has everything to do with concern. She said,

"You grew the beard."

"I did."

"Suits you."

London

Thomas Merton in his journal, written six months before his
Asian journey:

I realise that I have a past to break with—an accumulation of
inertia, wrong, foolishness, rot, junk. A great need of clarification,
of mindfulness, or rather, of no mind. A need to return to genuine
practice, right effort. Need to push on the great doubt. Need for
the spirit. Hang on to the clear light.

A freak electrical accident in Bangkok would kill him, mid-
way through the trip.

Aura of the lost.

In London, I tended to hang with the fallen. My aura of
eroding decay was a beacon to those travellers of the road less
survived. The drunks, dopers, cons, losers, dead angels. Come
to me, all ye who are lost, and I'll give you identification. Two

people I cultivated most. They belong on the fringe of the group I've outlined. Detective Sergeant Keegan was a pig. Worse, he was proud of it. Of murky Irish ancestry, he was based in south-east London, Brixton and Peckham being his beats of choice.

A loud vulgar bigot, he was coasting on dismissal from the force.

I was drinking on the Railton Road, nursing a hangover and the need to coke connect. The clientèle was predominantly black. Some whites, of course, who'd taken a wrong turn. The choice of booze was black rum with coke or without. Bob Marley was giving it large. A dreadlocks had offered to sell me a Rolex. I said,

"I don't do time."

"Yo, man, y'all be giving it to yer lady."

"No lady."

He threw back his locks, joined with Bob in "No Woman, No Cry".

I love that song.

Through the smoke, over the music, I'd heard guffawing. Glanced over my shoulder, saw a fat large man standing over a group of people. His suit jacket was lying on the floor, a pot belly had burst the buttons on his shirt. He'd a scarlet face, ruined in sweat. Mid-joke, he was gesturing obscenely. I muttered,

"Redneck."

Maybe louder than I intended, as the dread caught it, said,

"Yo no be messing with dat man."

I was a rum past caring, asked,

"Why's that?"

"Dat be Keegan. Dat be mujo trouble."

"Looks like a fat fuck to me."

The dread looked into my eyes, said,

"Yo be Irish, mon."

And fucked off. I signalled for more drink. It was a tad sweet for my taste, but went down like a smooth lie. I looked again at Keegan. He was singing now, "Living Next Door to Alice". I definitely heard the words *blow job* in there, which is some achievement, albeit a pointless one. I figured, he's one of two things, connected or cop. Not that they're mutually exclusive.

In my head, I was trying to remember the words to "Philosopher's Stone". Later, in my shitty bedsit, I'd attempt Marianne Faithful's version of "Madame George". Now that's a torch song.

A shoulder knocked against me and I spilled my drink, went,

"What the fu . . . ?"

Heard,

"Sorry, pal."

Turned to look into Keegan's face; sorry he wasn't. His actual words carried the sense of "screw you". He gave me the look, calculated, said,

"You're a cop."

"Not any more."

"An Irish cop. Well, fuck me . . . the Garda Chikini."

"Síochána."

"You what?"

"The pronunciation, you have it arseways."

For a horrible moment, I thought he was going to hug me. The thought danced round his eyes, faded, then,

"I love the Irish; well, some of the buggers anyway."

"Why?"

He gave a huge laugh. Heads turned, then away. Everything about him shouted animal, redneck, ludrimawn. But the laugh, you could forgive him lots on that. Came from way down and was sprinkled with graft and pain. He said,

"I had a holiday in Galway once, it was the races, but I never saw one bloody horse."

"I'm from Galway."

"You're having me on."

No one claims to be from there; you either are or you aren't. I knew I could shut down the whole deal right there and then, simply say,

"We don't like the English."

Maybe it was his laugh or the rum or even blame Brixton. I put out my hand, said,

"I'm Jack Taylor."

He shook, said,

"Keegan."

"Nothing else?"

"Unless you count Detective Sergeant."

He whistled to a woman; she sashayed over. No amount of rum would ever call her pretty. What she oozed was sex, lashings of it. He put his hand on her arse, asked,

"What's your name again, darling?"

"Rhoda."

"Rhoda, this is Jack Taylor, on undercover work for the Irish guards."

She gave an encompassing smile. She'd heard every tired line a parade of tired men ever pedalled. He slapped her arse, said,

"Go powder your nose, hon. This is guy stuff."

He watched her walk away, then asked,

"So Jack . . . want to ride that?"

London offers nigh on most things a person could crave. E.B.
White wrote of New York,

"Above all else, it offers you the chance to be lucky."

London doesn't quite make the same pitch, but it's in the neighbourhood. It never ceases to surprise. I wanted education.

My reading, expansive if not exhaustive, was haphazard. I wanted it formalised. Enrolled in night classes at London College. Taking literature and philosophy. At least I had a beard. Got a scarf in Oxfam and I was in the student mode. I wasn't the oldest, but I certainly appeared the most battered. London in November is a rough deal. Walking up Ladbroke Grove with that wind howling in your face, you are deep frozen. My bedsit was the last word in forlorn. A bed, a chair, electric heater and a shower. Oh yes, a hot plate. It had flock wallpaper, I kid you not. To compound the misery, I'd been reading Patrick Hamilton, *Hangover Square*.

Grim fare. He wrote, "To those whom God has deserted is given a gas fire in Earls Court." I could have hacked Earls Court.

There is a magical Irish word, *sneachta*. Pronounce it "shneackta", heavy on the guttural. It means snow. My first night of college, there were shitfuls of that. Harsh and unyielding. I was wearing black 501s, thermals, work boots, plaid shirt, denim jacket. Over that, I'd the leather coat and a watchcap. Still I was cold. Remember *Hill Street Blues,* the undercover guy who yelled "dogbreath" at perps? That's how I looked. Hardly enticing, yet I scored. Leastways, I thought I did. Nothing was further from my mind. Ann Henderson, in Galway, had crushed my heart. I didn't believe I had the mileage for another woman.

The lecturer was a prick. Bearded, too. He treated us like shite. I could care. He was mouthing about Trollope and I tuned out. At least it was warm. I'd clocked a dark-haired woman to my left. Aged in early forties with a strong face, sallow skin. Beneath a heavy parka, I surmised a rich body. She'd caught my eye, lingered, moved on. Class over, the guy was handing out assignments. The woman turned to me, said,

"*Guten Tag, Gedichte und Briefe zweisprächig.*"

"What?"

"Emily Dickson, her poems."

"I'll take your word for it."

She put out her hand, said,

"Kiki."

You immediately betray your age if you think "Kiki Dee". I said,

"Jack Taylor."

"So, Jack Taylor, would you join me for a drink?"

"I'll try."

She had an accent like a European who's learnt English in America. Not unpleasant.

There's a certain grandeur about English pubs. It's entirely different from the Irish animal. I hate to be the one to voice it, but they seem cosy. They did after all give us the term *snug*. Battened against the cold, we didn't speak the short distance to the pub. Once inside, we thawed in every sense of the word. She stood before an open fire, began to unwrap. I began to unravel. I hadn't had a line in four days. Not abstinence but my dealer got busted. The sniffles had nothing to do with temperature. I was cold, within and without, asked,

"What'll it be?"

"Oh, hot toddies, am I correct?"

"Are you ever?"

The barman/governor was elephants. The giveaway: blasted face, tired suit and too tight sovereign rings. He bellowed,

"And a good evening to you, sir."

"Um, right, couple of hot ones, better make them large . . . Oh, and whatever you're having yourself."

The beauty of the English system, drinking on duty. Had cost me my career. He had a large brandy, saying,

"I don't mind if I do."

Kiki was sitting almost in the fire. I said,

"You're hot."

"You wish."

I'm too old for powerhouse sex. But right there, right then,
I felt the ghost of it. Handed her the drink, said,

"*Sláinte.*"

"Excuse me?"

"It's Irish."

"It's lovely."

Usually I don't fuck with whiskey. No ice, no water, straight
as an angel. Those hot ones though, they were good. We got
another round, could feel the warmth to my toes. I asked,

"Where are you from?"

"Hamburg."

I'm sure there is a wise, not to mention pithy, reply, but I
couldn't summon it. My mind locked on *Fawlty Towers* with
"don't mention the war". I said,

"Ah."

She studied me closely, then,

"Fifty-three."

"What?"

"You are fifty-three."

Now I could hear the German, almost, *you will be fifty-three.*
I said,

"Forty-nine."

She didn't believe me. The oddest thing was happening. In my
head, I could hear the Furey Brothers with "When You Were
Sweet Sixteen". Not just a snatch, the whole song. For a moment,
it drowned out everything. I could see Kiki's lips moving but
hear nothing. Shook my head and it ebbed. She was saying,

"Would you sleep with me?"

Another tinker was killed. I'd slept late, woke in disorientation.
Where the hell was I? A comfortable bed, clean room, chintz
curtains. Hidden Valley. Shit, I was a home owner. I liked the
feeling. Took a slow shower, and with a tolerable hangover, I
wasn't hurting. Dressed in trainers, Brixton Academy sweatshirt. Went barefoot to get the benefit of those wood floors.
Did some eggs over easy and, bonus, real coffee. The kitchen
smelled good. I'd splashed on some Harley and blended in.

Got the radio tuned in and it was an old rock hour. Heard
Chicago and Supertramp. Did me.

The doorbell went. Opened it to Sweeper. Rage writ large,
he shouted,

"Did you hear?"

"Hear what?"

"Another one of our people has been killed."

"Oh, God."

He stormed in. I closed the door, resolved to proceed with caution. He was staring at my eggs. I asked,

"Get you something?"

"Tea, please."

He took a seat and produced a cigarette. Not a packet, just one crumpled fag. I passed him the Zippo and he said,

"Took me six months to quit."

Then he lit up. I got him his tea, fired up a red. My eggs had congealed. He said,

"I spoiled your breakfast."

"No worries, I hate eggs."

I didn't push for details, let him come to it. He said,

"Sean Nos was my nephew. I bought him his first van. Last night, he was found naked in the Fair Green; his hand was chopped off."

"Jesus."

"Left him to bleed to death."

He reached down and touched an Adidas holdall. I hadn't noticed it. He slid the bag along the floor, said,

"Open it."

"I don't think so."

"Open it, Mr Taylor."

I hunkered down, took a deep breath, then pulled back the zip. Saw the bloodied hand. The awful curse of observation. Even as my stomach churned, my mind ticked off details. The nails were clean, a thick wedding band on his wedding finger, black hair near the savage incision. I stood up, the kitchen spun. Turned round, got the cold tap going, put my head under it.

How long I don't know. Then Sweeper was handing me a towel, asking,

"Need a drink?"

I nodded. Saw the bag was closed and back by the chair. Sweeper pushed a mug into my hands. Took a slug. Brandy. The last time I had that, I woke up in the mental hospital at Ballinasloe. If I could get upstairs for a moment, I'd follow it with a line of coke. Fuck, lots of lines. My stomach warmed and I felt the artificial calm spread. Sweeper shook one of my cigarettes free, lit it and put it in my mouth. I said,

"OK, thanks, I'm all right."

Sweeper made more tea and said,

"It was left on my doorstep. One of my children could have opened it."

I knew it was pointless but made the play, asked,

"The guards, have you called them?"

He made a hissing noise through his teeth, like a spit articulated, asked,

"Did you yourself not meet with the top man himself only yesterday?"

"How did you know?"

"You work for me, it is my business to know how you conduct that work."

I wasn't real hot on "You work for me", no better opportunity to get that squared away. Put the mug down, said,

"We better get something straight, pal. I'm helping you out. I don't work for you; you are not my boss; I am not an employee. Are we clear?"

He gave a thin smile.

"You are a proud man, Jack Taylor. I understand pride. Here, take this."

He produced a cloth bundle. I said,

"You unwrap it."

He did. It was a 9mm Browning, Hi-Power. He said,

"It's the push-button release, see?"

He flicked his hand and the clip popped out. He continued,

"There are thirteen shots, one in the chamber. Here is the safety. To check it's on, cock the hammer."

He put it down on the table. I asked,

"And I'm supposed to do what exactly with it?"

"For protection."

"No, thanks, I don't do guns."

He rewrapped the weapon, moved to the sink and opened the press beneath. Reaching behind the pipes, he inserted the package, said,

"You never know."

"Have you any idea who'd want to kill your people?"

"Watch the news. Everybody hates the tinkers."

"That's a help."

I needed a suit and I needed to connect. Oxfam has priced
itself out of the market. In London, once, I'd gone to their
branch at High Street, Kensington. Jackets were chained like
the most paranoid Regent Street outlet. What's that about?
No, thanks. Went to Age Concern, found a dark blue, looked
too big but I could bulk up. Pack the gun and any suit would
fit. The price was a fiver with a navy shirt and worsted tie. The
assistant, English of course, said,

"Sorry it's so expensive."

"Are you serious?"

She was.

"It's brand new, you see, so we had to make it a little dearer."

I considered. Sure she was English, but they can do humour.
I said,

"Daylight robbery."

Huge smile then.

"Tell you what, I'll add a new hankie."

"My cup overflows."

Shoes I had. Kiki had bought me a pair of Weejuns. Next, it was time to score. I hated what I had to do, but the devil drives. Rang Cathy. She answered with a breezy,

"Jack."

I said,

"I need your help, girl."

"Of course, Jack, what do you need?"

"A name."

"Oh, Jack."

She knew. I guess she'd been through the hard station. I let some plead into my voice.

"I'm hurting, Cathy."

I waited, what else could I do? Standing in a phone box, holding my blue suit, like a guard on holidays. Then,

"Stewart."

And gave me the address. I asked,

"Will he be home?"

"He's always home."

Click. I held the dead phone. She wouldn't tell Jeff, but I had trod on our friendship. We'd survive, but I had seriously tarnished it. Went to the place, near the canal. The house looked normal. No shingle outside proclaiming "Drug Dealer". I rang the bell. The door was opened by a bank clerk. Leastways, he had the moneyed eyes. I asked,

"Stewart?"

"Cathy rang; come in."

An ordinary sitting room. There weren't flying ducks on the wall, but you get the picture. There was a framed *Desiderata*. Stewart said,

"Get you anything?"

"Yes, a gram of coke."

He gave a polite laugh, so I had to ask,

"You're not with the Bank of Ireland by any chance?"

"Hardly. I know you though."

"Yes?"

"Jack Taylor, ex-cop . . . you were in the papers last year."

"Stew, where are we on the coke?"

He excused himself, then returned with a brown envelope. The country was awash in them. He said,

"There's one and a half."

"Great, what's the damage?"

It was steep. As he let me out, he said,

"Call any time."

London by-law:

"No gypsy, hawker, beggar, rogue or vagabond shall enter the burial ground."

The funeral was massive and probably the biggest I've seen.
God knows I've seen a few. Sometimes, I feel like an old cemetery, laden with coffins. There is nothing like the funeral of a
tinker. It almost beggars belief. If there be truth in nothing in
your life becomes you like the leaving of it, then they score
heavily on all fronts. Descriptions like show-stopper, showpiece, showboat don't come close. The first thing to know is
expense doesn't matter. Secondly, you will almost never expe-
rience such an outpouring of grief. Arab women used to have
the lock on public demonstrations of sorrow. Not even close to
the women of travelling stock. It's not that they rend their gar-
ments: they lacerate their very souls. Dylan Thomas, when he
wrote of rage against the dying of the light, would have wit-
nessed his words personified.

I was relieved it was the Bohermore Cemetery because none
of my crowd is buried there. We're planted in Rahoon with

Nora Barnacle's dead lover. One of those days, I'd have to go visit.

Walking behind the hearse is a custom almost obsolete. Not that day. Sweeper came over, said,

"I got you a lift."

"I'll walk."

He was very pleased. At the graveside, various travellers shook my hand, clapped my shoulder. Word was out that I was OK. Neither settled community nor tinker, I was outlaw enough to be accepted. They said,

"God bless you, sir, thank you for your trouble. May Mary His Mother mind all belong to you."

Like that. Warmth articulated. I was coked enough and feeling no pain. Began to wander among the tombstones and there it was.

Tommy Kennedy

Librarian

1938–1989

Jesus, perilously close to the age I was now. I don't believe in omens, but coke does. I gave an involuntary shudder. Never heard Sweeper come up behind. He said,

"Jack."

I jumped two feet. He nodded at the headstone, said,

"He was a friend to my people."

"To me, too."

"The best go first."

"More's the Irish pity."

He gave me a look of near total compassion. That's not a

guy thing. We don't show that stuff. I didn't even want to hazard a guess as to what he thought of me. He said,

"There's a bit of a do at the hotel."

"Thanks, I'll be there."

"I know you will, Jack."

And he was gone. I put my trembling hand on Tommy's stone. Few men had ever shown as much kindness or taught me as much. I'd gone off to Templemore for guard training and forgotten all about him. To my eternal shame, he was dead for two years before I heard. God might forgive me, it's the business He's in. I won't. The presiding priest was my old nemesis, Fr Malachy. He was a friend of my mother's and loathed me. He smoked Major cigarettes, which had a brief fame when Robbie Coltrane smoked them in *Cracker*. True coffin nails, stronger than *poitín* and twice as lethal. He'd aged badly, but what smoker hasn't? Malachy approached me, said,

"You're back."

"True."

"I'd kill for a cig."

"You quit?"

"Good heavens, no, I left them in the vestry. The altar boys will steal them."

I offered the soft red pack. He gave me the look.

"And when did you start?"

"Forgive me, Father, you want one or not?"

He did, tore the filter off. I lit him up and he ate lungfuls, said,

"Shite."

"Nice language for a priest."

"I hate those things."

"So stop."

"Not cigarettes . . . funerals, especially this crowd."

"All God's children surely."

He slung the cig, said,

"Tinkers are nobody's children."

He was gone before I could respond.

Needless to say, I was first at the hotel. As a better man than me put it,

"Fair fuck to them for letting the tinkers in."

Recently the tinkers had hit back after years of discrimination, successfully suing pubs that denied access. The publicans had to regroup. As someone who's been barred from most establishments, my heart does not bleed. I stepped up to the counter. The barman looked like Robbie Williams. I could only hope his manner was different. He said,

"Good afternoon, sir. Are you with the funeral party?"

"I am."

"The bar is free until two thirty. What can I get you?"

"A pint and a Jameson chaser."

"Would sir like to take a seat? I'll bring it over."

I nibbled at the peanuts. Of all things, I was thinking of two authors. Tommy Kennedy had introduced me to them. Walter Macken, as fine then as now, and Paul Smith. Time was, on my shelf were *Esther's Altar, The Stubborn Season* and my sad favourite, *Summer Sang in Me.* Not too long ago, I'd found his *The Countrywoman* in a Lambeth library. Published in 1961, for me, it beats hands down either *Strumpet City* or *Angela's Ashes.*

Through Paul Smith, I discovered Edna St Vincent Millay, a mega bonus. The barman bought the drinks, said,

"Good health."

"Whatever."

The pint was as near perfect as I'd experienced. Got to agree with Flann O'Brien, "A pint of plain is your only man." Washed over the cocaine like a rosary. As a young guard, I went to see Eamonn Morrissey in *The Brother* and I was supposed to see Jack McGowran in *Waiting for Godot*. Got pissed instead. What a mistake. Took a hit of the Jameson and was as close to heaven as it gets. The travellers began to trickle in. Sweeper came over, said,

"Don't be alone."

"Is that like an imperative? Tell me, what did you do with the hand?"

"Buried it."

I took a hefty swig of the drink. Burned like a bastard, which was good. The place was hopping now. I said,

"Great crowd."

"We honour our own. No one else will."

"Sweeper, don't take this the wrong way, but I need to know what to call ye."

"I don't understand."

"Travellers, tinkers, gypos . . . what? I'm very uncomfortable with *tinkers*."

"It's what they call us."

"I didn't ask you that, did I? What do I term you?"

"The clans."

"Hey, that's good."

A faraway look came into his eyes. He said,

"After the Great Hunger, if the clans fell out, they'd set fire to each other's abodes, so we got fired."

A number of voices called him and he snapped back to the present, said,

"I must away."

"Away to the clans."

He gave the small smile. I had another drink and realised I felt at ease among them. I could have drunk me a river but I had to keep some semblance of focus. Told myself,

"The case is straightforward. All I have to do is find out who and why."

Finishing the whiskey, I thought,

"Fuck the who. I'll settle for why."

I stood in the Fair Green. Look north, there was the Simon Community. I was but a few drinks from a bunk there. If they'd have me. Behind me was the lure of the clans. Oh boy did it beckon, entreat, calling,

"Come back, get wasted, we'll mind you."

I'm sure they would, mind me, that is. Of course, I headed east, past at least four pubs where if not welcome, I would at least be tolerated. You can't say fairer than that. Always, once I get a certain ration of drink down, I get the munchies. Only for chips in newspaper, doused in vinegar, smelling to high heaven, heaven in measured doses.

Echoes of a childhood I wish I'd had. As a child the greatest comfort was the prospect of chips on a Friday night. School was out for the weekend, there was a match on Sunday, and you had a sixpence to go to the chipper. When the time finally arrived, it almost never disappointed. You galloped up to the chip shop, joined the queue and absorbed that magical aroma of deep fat and vinegar. You nearly swooned from expectation; then your turn came and you ordered,

"A single to go with salt and vinegar."

They came wrapped in newspaper and were too hot to eat, so you buried your nose in the smell. Of all your promises, you most pledged to live on chips when you were an adult. Among the many reasons I hate fast food joints is they deprive children of the mystery of the chipper. There is still a place in Bohermore that sells "singles", and that's where I bought them now. I held the hot package in my hands as I moved along St Bridget's Terrace. Then crossed at the new luxury apartments and hit the crest of the hill. Right above Hidden Valley, you can see the Corrib and the sheer stretch of it. At night, the lights of the college sprinkle across the water and arouse such yearning, but for what?

I still don't know.

At the house, I followed the honoured tradition of fumbling for my keys. I heard,

"Excuse me?"

Turned to take an iron bar smack in my mouth. Felt my teeth go, heard a voice say,

"Get him in the alley."

It runs alongside the house. I was dragged and then took a ferocious kick in the balls. Up came the chips and booze, heard,

"Aw, for fuck's sake, he's puked all over me."

"Break his nose."

He did, with the bar. That was about it. I lay slumped against the wall. A voice beside my ear,

"Like to hang with the tinkers, do you?"

Then an intake of breath and he kicked me on the side of the head. I blacked out. When I came to, I don't know was it minutes or hours. An elderly couple passed and she said,

"The cut of him, it's scandalous."

If I could, I'd have shouted,

"What do you expect? I'm a tinker."

Eventually, I got inside, went to the sink and spat. Teeth and blood tumbled out. I got to the front room and a bottle of Irish, drank from the neck. The raw alcohol lacerated my torn gums, but it got past them. My suit was destroyed, the blue shirt in shreds. Despite what the movies show, it takes some strength to rip a shirt. I found my crumpled cigs and fired up. Held the heavy Zippo like a talisman. More whiskey, better. After much searching, I found Sweeper's number, then an age to focus till finally,

"Hello?"

"It's Jack, help me."

I passed out. When I next opened my eyes, I was lost. In bed, in pyjamas, first thought,

"Oh fuck, not hospital."

If hospitals gave air miles, I could have travelled extensively. Heart lurch, a figure near the door. Focused, my head howled. It was Sweeper, asleep in a chair. Keeping the night watch. I couldn't feel a hangover. Why couldn't I? Worrying. Sweeper held the 9mm in his lap. I better not make any sudden moves. Gave a small cough. He stirred, and I asked,

"Where's my hangover?"

He shook himself, seemed surprised to find the gun, laid it on the floor, said,

"You're full of painkillers."

My mouth was numb but not hurting. Numb I could hack. Asked,

"Who put me to bed?"

Half smile then.

"We found you on the floor. You were in bad shape, my friend. Got a doctor and he worked on you. That was two days ago."

"Jesus."

"The clan have guarded you in shifts. You will, of course, need a dentist."

"I need tea."

He got up, and I nodded at the gun. He said,

"If you'd been carrying this, you wouldn't be toothless."

"I was carrying chips. If I'd had that, they'd have made me eat it."

"They surprised you?"

"They bloody amazed me."

He went to do tea things, and I got cautiously out of bed. Woozy but functional, I moved slowly towards the bathroom, avoiding the mirror. I've never been an oil painting, but without teeth, I was the total descent into ugliness. Told myself,

"Gives character to your face."

Sure. That and a 9mm, maybe people wouldn't fuck with me. When I finally got downstairs, I had on an NUI sweatshirt, faded 501s. My balls were black and blue and swollen. Managed to drink some tepid tea, skipped the toast. Sweeper passed over some red and grey capsules, said,

"Keep the pain at a distance."

I was thinking coke, possible with a broken nose? He said,

"I removed the cocaine lest the guards come."

When I didn't answer, he said,

"Tiernans."

"What?"

"Brothers, the ones who did you. They hate tinkers. They've gone to ground, but when they surface . . . I'll let you know."

The end, for all anyone could tell,
Was a conversation; polite, civilised
Almost banal; you had coffee with milk
No sugar. That was your
Customary choice. Nothing strange in that.
But, I had tea . . .
An unaccustomed choice;
Appropriate for an upheaval.

Jeff O'Connell

Apart from a visit to the dentist, I didn't venture out much over
the next few weeks. Stayed home, stayed semi-pissed. The dentist went,

"Argh . . ."

This wasn't good. He asked,

"What happened?"

"Rugby scrum."

He gave me the look but let it slide. An hour and a half in the chair as he did horrendous things. My mouth was so full of instruments, I could have started a DIY. When we took a break, I said,

"Don't tell me any of the procedures."

"I've gotten most of the fragments out and . . ."

"Whoa, Doc . . . trust me, I truly do not want to know."

Back in the chair, more excavation. Finally he did the impressions, said,

"Should be able to fit you in a fortnight."

"Can't you dance something temporary in there?"

Shaking his head, he said,

"Trust me, Mr Taylor, when the anaesthetic wears off, even your tongue is going to seem too much."

As I prepared to leave, he asked,

"Have you medical insurance?"

"Nope, that and no teeth: the Irish male in all his glory."

"Well, at least you've kept your sense of humour. I think you're going to need it."

"Thanks, Doc, I wish I could say it's been a pleasure."

"I'd ease up on the rugby for a bit."

During my last case, I'd been involved with a guard named Brendan Flood. He'd kicked the bejaysus out of me, broken the fingers of my left hand. That was the first time I met him. Then he got religion and a massive change of allegiance. Actually solved the case and led me to killing my best friend. What they call a colourful relationship. I'd kept his number and rang him that evening.

"Hello?"

"Brendan, it's Jack Taylor."

Long pause, then deep intake of breath.

"You're back."

"I am."

"They never found your friend."

"No, no, they didn't."

"What can I do for you, Jack?"

"Your information was gold before: I wonder if I might prevail on you further?"

"As long as it concurs with the Lord."

"Still a believer, eh?"

"Yes, Jack, the Lord believes in you, too."

"Glad to hear it."

I told him about the killing of the tinkers. He asked,

"The guards are not actively pursuing this?"

"That's why I'm calling you. Can you help?"

"Give me your number, I'll ask around."

"Great, but be discreet."

"The Lord is my discretion."

Click.

I was drinking Robin Redbreast. Christ, if that isn't a blast from the fifties. My father would have a glass with his slice of Christmas cake. God knows, as my mother baked it, you'd need all the help available. He was a good man. My mother is a walking bitch, then and now. I hadn't heard light nor hair of her in over a year. Maybe she was dead. She adored my one outstanding credential: my failure. With such a son, she could be seen to endure. The woman was born to martyrdom, but only with an audience. Pay per view.

My expulsion from the guards, my drinking, my non-starter life: she couldn't have wished for more. Bit down hard on this line of territory. Shit, what was I playing at? Picked up the phone, rang Kiki. This number I had memorised.

"It's Jack."

"Jack, how are you? Why haven't you called? When can I come?

"Jeez, slow down, I'm fine and . . . I miss you."

"So, can I come?"

"Of course, but give me two weeks."

"Why, Jack?"

"Cosmetic reasons."

"I don't understand."

"Look, good news, I have a house and a job."

"But, Jack, you know I need my own space."

I wanted to shout,

"If you need your own space, why the fuck come to Ireland?"

But stayed with it, said,

"Stay here for a few days till you get acclimatised."

"Ireland is so different?"

"Trust me, after fifty years, I'm still adapting."

"I can come in two weeks?"

"Absolutely."

"And, Jack, do you love me?"

"Sure."

"I love you, too."

Put the phone down and pondered the conversation. No, I didn't love her. Blamed the Robin Redbreast.

The morning of my new teeth, I was one happy private investigator. Remember Dire Straits? They'd been doing fine, cooking, pulling the hip and the straight alike. No mean feat. Then Lady Di announced they were her favourite band and wallop. *Sayonara*, suckers. Now they got bracketed with Duran

Duran, and there's no coming back from there. "Money for Nothing" sounded what it was—smug. Like many rock stars, Mark Knopfler paid tribute to humility and started The Notting Hill Billies. Yes, we're just ordinary blokes. That group went down the ordinary toilet. I was running all this trivia to keep my mind distracted as the dentist slotted in my new molars. He said,

"They'll take a little getting used to."

"Like the new Ireland."

He smiled and told me the cost. I went,

"Jeez, could I just rent them, you think?"

He didn't.

All along Shop Street, I smiled, giving those teeth exposure. I heard a wino say,

"That ejit has drink taken."

Nearly went into Grogan's, my old favourite pub. Sean, the grouchy proprietor, had owned most of my heart. He'd been murdered, too, and because of me. That fair dented my smile. When I got to Hidden Valley, Sweeper was waiting at the kitchen table. I said,

"Be free, drop in or out of my place anytime, don't feel you have to phone ahead."

He gave the turned-down mouth expression, said,

"Teeth, eh?"

I gave him the full neon. He nodded, asked,

"How's your balls?"

"The swelling's gone."

Head shake, then,

"I didn't mean the actual set."

"Oh, you meant metaphorically. Give me my coke back, I'll fight legions."

"Just two, the Tiernans; they've surfaced."

My gut tightened. He reached in his suit pocket. Sweeper always wore a dark suit, white shirt. Most times, he appeared more Greek waiter than traveller. He produced a small leather pouch. Leather thong to fit round the neck. I asked,

"What's with the suits? It's not as if you have to be at an office."

Sad smile then.

"I have to stay respectable. They expect us to be tinkerish, but I give the lie to their assumptions."

"OK, but don't you ever want to just kick back, hang loose?"

With his hand he dismissed this nonsense, tapped the pouch, said,

"Open it."

"You're kidding. Knowing you, it's probably a shrunken head."

Now finally he laughed, said,

"You're in the neighbourhood."

Turning the pouch up, he shook it. Four bloodied teeth rolled on the table. I went,

"Ah, fuck."

"In case you need motivation for the brothers."

He scooped them up, put them back and handed me the bag.

Reluctantly, I pulled the thong over my head, settled the thing inside my shirt, said,

"Now I'm Brando, *Apocalypse Now*."

He stood up, said,

"I'll collect you at seven. Bring the weapon."

"What will I wear, it being a revenge number?"

He considered, then,

"Something cold."

That lunchtime I got parcel post. No stamp and unfranked, opened it up. The coke. I said aloud,

"Good on you, Sweeper."

Laid out a line. My nose was healing but still hurt like a bastard. Managed three hits. After a two and a half week layoff, it hit like thunder. Thank God. My gums froze, and I could feel that icy tingle down my throat, froze my brain. Now I could face a mirror. Not good. The nose was tilted to the left. Perhaps the next breakage might realign it. There would be another, always was. Deep blue shadows under my eyes, they'd accessorise a guard's uniform. New ridges along the corner of my mouth. How frigging old was I getting? Not old enough to ever like George Michael. Flashed the smile, solid. A 100-watt beacon in the wasteland. Maybe my teeth could go out alone. A jingle from my childhood:

"You'll wonder where the yellow went/when you brush your teeth with Pepsodent."

Ah.

The coke was cranking hard. I had to go out. Show my

twenty-year-old smile in the face of fifty. Almost a haiku, it was definitely a shame. Put on a white shirt, slacks and the Weejuns. Next the London leather, and I was the oldest swinger in town. The pouch bounced against my chest like the worst of bad news. Coming out into the light, I couldn't believe the sun was bright. No warmth but I could fake that. A neighbour said,

"We lost the replay."

"We did?"

"Can't beat them Kerry bastards."

"Maybe next year."

"Maybe shite."

My kind of neighbour. I went to Zhivago Records. Declan looked up, said,

"You're back."

"How astute."

"How what?"

"Never mind. I need the King."

"Elvis?"

"Is there another?"

"Greatest Hits?"

"Exactly."

"CD?"

"Declan, far be it from me to tell you your business, but if the customer's over forty, it's not a CD."

"You need to get digital."

"I need to get laid. Now can I have the record?"

"Jeez, Jack, you're a touchy bastard. What happened to your nose?"

"I told a fellah to get digital."

He knocked a few quid off, so I forgave him most.

I knew I should visit the cemetery, back all this time and not one visit. Did I feel guilty? Oh God, yes. Guilty enough to go? Not quite.

Met an Irish Romanian named Chaz. He used to be fully Romanian but had gone native. He asked,

"Fancy a pint?"

"Sure."

We went to Garavan's. Unchanged and unspoilt. I took a corner seat and Chaz got the round. I took out my cigs and fired up. Chaz came with the pints, said,

"*Sláinte.*"

"Whatever."

He helped himself from the Marlboro pack, used the Zippo. He examined it, said,

"This is hammered silver."

"So?"

"A gypsy made this."

"Got that right."

"Sell it to me."

"It's on loan."

"Lend it to me."

"No."

The pints went down easy, and I ordered a fresh batch. I

took a good look at Chaz; he was wearing an Aran sweater with army fatigues. I asked,

"How's it going?"

"I'm hoping for a grant from the Arts Council."

"For what?"

"I don't know yet, but I'll think of something."

"How can you lose?"

"You know, Jack, in Ireland, the people are not fond of Romanians."

"Sorry to hear it."

"But in Galway it's different."

"Good."

"No, in Galway they hate us."

"Ah."

"Lend me a fiver, Jack."

I did. Said "See you soon" and headed off. Walked slap into my mother. She looked above my head, which read pub. Hardly a halo. Her skin was, as ever, unlined, as if life never touched it. Nuns have the same deal. Estée Lauder take note: check out nuns. The eyes, you look into hers, you see the Arctic, ice blue. Always the same message:

"I'll bury you."

She said,

"Son."

Aware of my Guinness breath, broken nose, I said,

"How are you?"

"You're back."

"I am."

Then silence. Her type thrive on it. Reared on the game, backed by the booze, I could play. Waited. She caved. Said,

"I could buy you a cup of tea."

"I don't think so."

"The GBC, they do lovely scones."

"Not today."

"You didn't think to write?"

Same old tune, whine on. I said,

"Oh, I thought to write. I just didn't think to write to you."

Landed home. She sighed. They ever put together an Olympic event for that, she's a shoo-in. All the time people hurrying by, oblivious to us. I said,

"I have to go."

"That's all you have for your own mother?"

"No, actually, I have this."

Ripped the pouch from my neck, put it in her hand. I was going to add,

"You can put it with my father's heart."

Why gild the lily?

"Summer sang in me."

Edna St Vincent Millay

Sweeper collected me on time. In a white van, spotlessly clean. I got in the passenger seat, four young men in the back wearing black tracksuits. I said,

"Lads."

They said nothing. Sweeper put the van in gear, eased into the late evening traffic. I said,

"I got you a present."

He was well surprised, went,

"What?"

I passed over the package. He undid the bag, one eye on the road, said,

"Elvis Presley!"

"Like you, he's the boss."

Chorus of amused approval from the back. We were turning at Nile Lodge. He said,

"They live in Taylor's Hill."

"Must have a few bob."

He looked at me, asked,

"No relation?"

"What?"

"The Hill . . . Taylor's?"

I shook my head, said,

"I'm the wrong side of the tracks."

He mulled over that, asked,

"You ready?"

"For what?"

"Doing as you're told."

"Mmmmmmmmm, that's always been a problem."

"Try."

"Well, I've always been trying, God knows."

The quiet section of the Hill, not a pound from Threadnee-dle Road, we stopped, pulled into a lay-by. Sweeper nodded and the lads slipped out like phantoms. I asked,

"The Tiernans, they own this house or what?"

He gave a grim smile.

"Inherited, neither of them married. They get videos, cur-ries, lager and party on. No women. The cream of Irish man-hood, batchelors and proud of it."

I said,

"You're married, aren't you?"

"Yes, with young children, but don't talk of family now."

"OK."

"When the light flashes, we go."

"One last question."

"What?"

"Why do they call you Sweeper?"

"We clean chimneys."

"Oh, and as we speak, what are the lads doing?"

"That's two questions."

"You're counting?"

"The lads are preparing the way."

"I see."

"You will."

The light flashed. I had the 9mm in the waistband at my back, like in the best movies. Jeez, I didn't even know was it loaded. Didn't feel it was the time to ask. The house was mock Tudor, acres of ivy obliterating the front. The door was opened, and I followed Sweeper. Down a hall littered with spares, bicycles, stripped down engines. Into a huge living room. The lads were in possession. Two sat on a fat guy on the floor. A skinnier version was sitting in an armchair, a knife held to his throat. Both the men were in shorts and singlets. Sweeper said,

"The fat one on the floor is Charlie; the other, the brains, is Fergal."

Hearing his name, Fergal smiled. A bruise was already forming on his cheek. He spat, said,

"Taylor, you stupid cunt."

The lad on the left smacked a fist in his ear. Rocked him, but the defiance stayed full. I said,

"Lads, move away."

They looked to Sweeper, who nodded. I took out the 9mm, moved over, asked,

"Fergal, is it?"

"Fuck you."

"Jeez, Ferg, easy with the language."

He felt he was almost back in control, said,

"See that gun, I'll ram it up your arse."

Charlie, on the floor, despite a bloodied face, cackled, shouted,

"You tell him, Fergal."

Emboldened, Fergal roared,

"What are you going to do, shithead?"

I said,

"First this . . ."

I turned and shot Charlie in the knee, continued,

"Then I'm going to castrate you."

Charlie shrieked, and I said,

"Gag him."

Fergal was afraid, sweat blinding him. I said,

"Watch."

Stuck the barrel in his nuts, asked,

"Anything else?"

"Oh, Christ, Taylor . . . please . . . it got out of hand, we're sorry."

I said,

"You owe me for a set of teeth."

"Sure, no problem. Jesus, anything you want. You like videos, we have brilliant films."

"I want your teeth."

Cracked the barrel into his mouth, bent down, said,

"I never want to hear from you again."

He nodded, holding his mouth. I turned to Sweeper, said,

"I'm done."

Back in the van, I tried to light a cig. Couldn't. Sweeper did it, stuck the filter in my mouth. He put the van in gear and we eased slowly out of there. After a time, Sweeper said,

"I thought you were going to do it, shoot his balls off."

I took a long hit, said,

"So did I."

Soft laughter from the back. I should have paid more attention to those lads. The fact that I didn't would cost me in a way I could never have imagined.

Kiki arrived on a wet afternoon. I took a cab to the airport to
meet her. The driver was saying,

"There's been positive dope testing at the Para-Olympics."

You can't encourage taxi drivers. Even the most non-committal grunt is interpreted as,

"You are so fascinating, please tell me all your opinions on everything immediately and never let me get a word in."

He was off.

"Now your regular Olympics, OK, we expect them to cheat. But your cripples and such, you think they'd have integrity, am I right?"

Next we'd get to whose fault it was. He asked,

"Know who I blame?"

"No idea."

"Your Arabs."

"Oh."

"They drug the water."

When we got to Carnmore, I asked,

"Can you wait?"

"Sure. You want me to come inside, grab a tea with you?"

"No."

As Kiki came through the gate, my heart did a minor chord. Not wild abandon, more a distant relative. She looked gorgeous. Navy jacket, faded blue cords. I said,

"You look gorgeous."

Put her arms round me, full kiss, said,

"Jack, you're blushing."

"That's mortification."

Got her bags, and to my relief, they were small. Not planning a long trip. Getting in the cab, I said,

"Don't mention sport."

As we pulled out, the driver said,

"There's been positive dope testing . . ."

At Hidden Valley, I was carrying Kiki's bags from the cab when the neighbour passed. He winked, said,

"You yoke."

The English might say "you rascal", but it hasn't the same flavour.

She loved the house. I got some drinks, said,

"*Sláinte.*"

"Oh, I like that word. I like you. What happened to your nose, your teeth?"

"A misunderstanding."

"Are you in trouble, Jack?"

"Of course not."

We went to bed. I wish I could say I delighted her. I didn't. She said,

"What's wrong, Jack?"

"Nothing, I'm just not used to you."

"Maybe the alcohol, the cocaine, they robbed you."

"No . . . Jeez, a few days, I'll be fine, you'll see."

Neither of us believed it. That evening, I said,

"Come and meet some friends."

We went to Nestor's. The sentry ignored us. Jeff was tending bar. I said,

"Jeff, this is Kiki, a friend from London."

She shot me a look. Jeff shouted for Cathy and asked,

"Can I get you something to say welcome to Ireland?"

"A small Guinness."

"I'll have a pint, Jeff."

Cathy arrived, curiosity writ large. Her pregnancy was very developed, and she and Kiki got into woman talk. We were sitting on stools, Cathy behind the bar with Jeff, when Cathy asked,

"Well, Jack, how come you kept this terrific woman a secret?"

Kiki looked at me, then asked Cathy,

"Jack hasn't told you?"

"No, nothing."

"I'm Jack's wife."

Even the sentry went,

"What?"

Jeff recovered first, went and got a bottle of champagne. Cathy remained stunned. Kiki said,

"I'm going."

I followed her outside, said,

"But they're preparing a celebration."

"I will need keys, Jack."

I handed over the spare set I'd been planning to give her later. She asked,

"Where do I ask for?"

I told her and she hailed a cab. I half hoped it was the Olympic guy. Then she was gone. Back in the bar, all stood waiting. I said,

"Better put the champagne on ice."

The sentry said,

"Their first row."

Cathy added,

"I doubt it."

I ordered a large Jameson, took my hard seat. Cathy brought it over, asked,

"Can I sit?"

"Sure."

I got a cig going, circled my drink. Cathy asked,

"Is whiskey a good idea?"

"Is marriage?"

"Good heavens, Jack, how come you never said?"

"I don't know. I think I thought it was a London thing. You know, come home, leave the bedsit, all that behind."

"But God . . . I mean . . . did you love her . . . what?"

"I was a little crazy over there."

"What a change."

"Yea, yea, anyway, I thought it would settle me. She has a doctorate in metaphysics."

"Is that supposed to tell me something? I can't even pronounce it."

"It's the study of being."

"Gee, Jack, that really clears it up for me."

"I thought she might see into my soul, see some redemption."

Cathy stood up, said,

"The baby's kicking, I'll have to lie down. You're going to have to stop the coke, you know that, don't you?"

"Sure."

A little later, a man came in, spotted me, walked over. He was familiar but that's all. He said,

"Jack."

"Yea?"

"I'm Brendan Flood."

"Of course. I'm not long married; it appears to have rattled me. A drink?"

"A mineral, please."

Got that squared away. Least he didn't ask for a straw. He had aged badly. Wearing a donkey jacket with the leather patches. Opened it to reveal a heavy silver cross. I said,

"I've a lighter from the same seam."

He shook his head, said,

"It does you no merit to mock."

"Sorry."

"It's not too late for repentance."

"Would it help if I knew metaphysics?"

"I am speaking of belief, Jack, of faith. Knowledge is the tool of Satan."

"How did you find me?"

At last a slight easing. He said,

"We were guards, Jack."

I signalled for another drink, and Brendan said,

"There is indeed a pattern to the deaths of those unfortunate men."

"Go on."

"All were found naked; a degree of savagery, mutilation is common to all. And each was in his late twenties, none over thirty."

"Anything else?"

"The guards have consigned it to family feuding."

"What do you think, Brendan?"

He sipped at his mineral. If it was giving him any pleasure, he was hiding it, said,

"I think someone is systematically stalking and killing young tinkers."

"Jesus."

"Don't take the Lord's name in vain. You might want to talk to Ronald Bryson."

"Who's he?"

"An English social worker with the Simon Community. They have a shelter in the Fair Green. All the bodies were found nearby."

I put my hand in my pocket, pulled out a wedge, laid it near his drink. He asked,

"What's that?"

"For your time, your help."

He considered, then pocketed it, said,

"I'll give it to the missions."

"Don't you have a family?"

"God is my family."

He stood up, said,

"So. Congratulations are in order."

"What?"

"You have a wife now."

"No, that was a rumour masquerading as fact."

"God mind you well, Jack."

Later, much later, Jeff said,

"You better go home, Jack."

"I don't want to go home. I want to stay here."

"You have a wife, go home. I think Cathy's going to have the baby real soon. I need some sleep."

"Right, call me when the time comes."

"Sure."

"Promise."

"I promise. Now go."

When I got to my front door, I checked for Tiernans. Nope, no warriors. Staggered inside, said,

"Kiki, you awake?"

Fumbled my way to the kitchen, checked the time. Three thirty in the morning. How did that happen? Thought,

"I'll do one line of coke, clear my head, then see if Kiki's up for some serious love-making."

I was smiling; this was a good plan. Kiki would learn I could be a stud. Just get me started, I could last as long as Sting. A note was propped up against the kettle. Beside it were the bullets from the 9mm. They shone as if they'd been polished. Before the note I decided to coke up a little more. Stashed in the fridge, between the Flora and the low fat yoghurt, keep it chilled. Got the line, a fatter one than planned, and snorted. Knocked me against the wall, felt like it blew a hole in my gut. I went,

"Phew-oh."

Then,

"Whoops, keep it low, folk trying to sleep."

My mind focused, I tiptoed to the note . . . maybe sneak up on it. It read,

Jack,

Not "Dear Jack". Already it was looking ominous. Read on.

I have checked into a hotel. I am going back to London tomorrow. You bastard, you humiliated me and still I love you. I do not want to see you. I found the weapon when I searched for detergent. You make me so afraid. My present to you I left on our . . . no . . . your bed.

Kiki

I said,

"Bummer."

And slumped on the floor. Late next morning, I came to with paranoia screaming at me. My neck was cramped, I'd been sick on my leather coat and my nose howled. Muttered,

"Could be worse."

Then I resaw the note. Trudged upstairs, and there on the bed was a parcel. Opened it to reveal brown Bally boots. Serious comfort. Kick the crap out of them and they came back, holding class. If I was to be buried in my boots, let them be Ballys. Came as close to weeping as self-pity will allow. Endured a shower, then put all the clothes in the wash, even the leather. Turned the mother on, thought,

"Too late for fabric softner."

The phone went. I put a cig together, picked up, went,

"Hello."

It wasn't Kiki, but heard,

"London calling."

"What? Keegan?"

"That's right, boyo."

"How'd you get my number?"

"Rang the guards, spoke to a prick named Clancy. He doesn't like you, mate."

"Good Lord, wow, I mean hello."

"Hello yourself. I have leave."

"Leave?"

"Holidays, squire. I'm going to hop a flight."

"Now?"

"You betcha. You want me to come, don't you?"

"Sure."

"OK then, eleven tonight, I'll be in that Quays pub."

"Tonight?"

"Get your skates on, pal; it's going to be a bumpy ride."

He hung up. I thought about his arrival, then thought,

"Why the hell not?"

And long before the final cry
A thin taut whisper
Filters down
To ask for one last song.

K.B.

If I dreamt, it was of nothing good. Woke in a coke sweat, mut-
tered,

"Incoming!"

Horror of horrors, reached for Kiki and touched the Bally
boots, whispered,

"Och, ochon."

Which is Irish for "Oh sweetfuck". Is it ever? The old *Jackie
Gleason Show*, in black and white, he'd begin each episode with
"How sweet it is." I crawled into the shower, got it to scald and
burned my way up. Checked the wardrobe and heard the
refrain the drugs used to whisper to Richard Pryor:

"Getting a little low, Rich."

Wore a white T-shirt—well, whiteish—the 501s, and pulled
on the new boots. Perfect, which was a pity as that made me so
guilty about Kiki. Alkies have to be the strangest animals on
the planet, like the song says, a walking contradiction. Kris

Kristofferson wrote the best lines of drinking despair. He was the personification of De Mello's "Awareness". If you really listen to "Sunday Morning Coming Down", it's the alky anthem. Particularly when you get the smell of someone frying chicken. That's close to the loneliest line I've heard. London, wet Sunday afternoon, the pubs are shut, you're battling that wind off Ladbroke Grove and, for an instant, a whiff of a home-cooked meal. You are seriously fucked.

Down to the kitchen, checked the time: eight forty-five. Brewed up some tea and dry toast, managed that. An impulse nagging at me. Figured I better make an attempt. Good old yellow pages. I began phoning.

"Hello?"

"Good evening, Imperial Hotel, how may we help you?"

"Do you have a . . . Mrs Taylor registered?"

"One moment, sir, I'll check."

For one awful moment, I feared my mother might come to the phone. Then,

"Sorry, sir, we don't have anyone by that name registered."

Click. I trawled through half a page. My tea got cold and the toast curled. Now there's a country song. Was phoning by rote when,

"Yes, sir, we did have a Mrs Taylor, but she checked out."

"Did she leave a forward?"

"I believe a cab took her to the airport."

I missed her. Loaded the wet clothes into the dryer, including the leather, said,

"Melt, see if I care."

My only other coat was Item 8234, my all-weather issue. They kept writing, demanding it back. The Mounties might always get their man, but the guards do not get their coat, not yet. Wrapped the coat tight. Didn't do the coke, didn't have a drink, but I could taste them. One final call; dialled, got,

"Simon Community, can I help?"

"May I speak to a Ronald Bryson?"

Heard a shout, an answer, then,

"Ron is off till noon tomorrow."

"Could I see him then?"

"He'll be here."

Click. Enough detective work for one day; time to party. Checked my wallet and headed out. Five minutes to Nestor's, how easy does it get? Decided to cut through St Patrick's Church, shake a few memories. Stopped at the grotto. If I was to pray, it should be for Kiki. Heard,

"Well, I never. Jack Taylor in prayer."

Fr Malachy, in all his smug glory. Even if I didn't like priests, I wouldn't like him. Ever. He was sucking the guts out of a dying cig. I said,

"Still smoking."

"I was just with your mother."

"Gee, that's a shock."

"Shock, is it? The poor woman is in deep trauma since she met you. To give her . . . teeth."

"My teeth."

He was raising his eyes in that "Lord give me strength" deal they learn at priest school. He said,

"She'll never be the better of it."

"Mmm, I'd say she'd recover."

"What on earth possessed you?"

"The drink, Father, the drink made me do it."

His right hand came up, automatic reflex when they're crossed. So many years they could safely lash out without repercussions. I smiled and he fought back the urge. I turned to look at the statue, asked,

"If I claimed it moved, would it help business?"

"You're a pup."

He pulled out the Majors, got one lit, dragged madly as if he could inhale the rage. I said,

"I have some good news for my mother."

"You're leaving town?"

"No, I got married."

"What?"

"But she's leaving town. In fact, she's already gone."

"You have a wife and she's gone already?"

"In a nutshell."

He flung the cig into the grotto, said,

"You're stone mad."

"But never boring, right, Malachy?"

"To hell with you."

And he stomped off, I called,

"That's not a blessing."

A local woman, passing, said,

"Good on you. That fellah's got too big for his boots."

I said the prayer for Kiki, albeit a short one.

In Nestor's, Jeff asked,

"Did you find her?"

"She's gone."

"Gone."

"Back to London."

"Jeez, Jack."

"Where's Cathy?"

"She's angry with you. Give her a few days."

He put up a pint, said,

"On the house."

"Thanks, Jeff."

"What's the plan?"

"I'm meeting Keegan."

"Who?"

"Detective Sergeant Keegan, London Metropolitan Police."

"In London?"

"No, in The Quays, in about an hour."

"Is it work?"

"He's a piece of work."

"Forget I asked, forget I asked anything."

The sentry was in place and he glared. I asked,

"What?"

"I liked your missus."

"Oh, God."

Heading down Shop Street. It was cold, but that didn't stop the street theatre. Muted. Dented but there. A juggler outside Eason's, a busker at Griffin's bakery, a Charlie Chaplin near Feeney's. A German couple asked,

"Where can we find the Krak?"

I waved my hands in the direction I'd walked, asked,

"What do you call that?"

The Quays was jammed. Above the tumult I could hear an English accent with,

"A hot toddy, love, and a pint of the black stuff."

Who else could it be? Chaz, my Romanian friend, came out of the crowd before I could call Keegan, said,

"Remember the fiver I lent you yesterday?"

"No, Chaz, I lent you."

"You sure?"

"Yes, but did you want another?"

"You're the best, Jack."

"Tell my wife."

Keegan was wearing a white sweatshirt with the logo *"Póg mo thóin",* bright red golf pants and a Blackpool souvenir hat which begged,

"Kiss me quick."

He shouted,

"Jack Taylor, me best mate."

Shoved a pint in my hand, said,

"There's hot ones on the counter and drink, too."

I thought,

"Am I up for this? Is anyone up for this?"

I asked,

"Where's your luggage?"

"In Jury's."

"You booked in there? But I have a place."

"Yea, that's great, mate, but I might be shagging."

Argue that. I went with the flow. Keegan is a force of nature, raw, ugly, powerful and unstoppable. There's a nightclub on Eyre Square called Cuba. I don't think there's a Gaelic translation. Two o'clock, I'm there with Keegan and two women he's cajoled. They appear to love him. He puts his arm round one, says,

"Jack, I love this country."

"It sure loves you."

"Too true, son; I'm a Fenian bastard."

To hear that in an English accent is to have lived a very long time. The manager came over and I thought,

"Uh-oh."

Wrong. It was to offer complimentary champagne. Keegan said,

"Bring it on, squire. We'll have black pudding for breakfast."

I'd resigned myself to the Twilight Zone. Over the next hour I told Keegan the events of the past weeks. He said,

"You mad bastard, I love you."

Whatever else they label him, judgemental he wasn't. He flashed a wad of notes at the girls, said,

"Trust my instincts, but you'd like sticky drinks with the umbrellas . . . am I right?"

He was and they adored him. He turned back to me, said,

"The dark-haired one, I want to ride the arse off that . . . OK?"

"Um . . . yes."

"The quiet one, you have her, OK?"

"Thanks, I think."

Then he got serious. All the yahoo-ism, vulgarity, the Hunter S. Thompson shenanigans dropped in a second. He said,

"Jack, I'm a good cop, only thing I can do, but the bastards are trying to get rid of me. Only a matter of time till they bounce me."

"I've been there."

"So, I'm only going to say one thing, mate."

"OK."

"Stick with the case. Nothing else matters."

"I will."

Then he clicked back to John Belushi, said to the girls,

"So, who wants to lick my face first?"

Next morning, opened my eyes, did a double take. A girl beside me. Last night came flooding back, at least as far as Cuba. She looked about sixteen. I moved the sheet, and oh fuck, she was naked. Jail bait. She stirred, woke and smiled, said,

"Hi."

I've had worse beginnings. I answered,

"Hi, yourself."

She cuddled into me, said,

"This is lovely."

Then pulled back, said,

"Thank you for taking advantage."

"Um . . ."

"You're a real gent."

Go figure. The heat from her was stirring me, and I said,

"Let me get some tea, toast."

"Can we have breakfast in bed?"

"Course we can."

"Jack, you're the greatest."

Out of bed, I was starkers. Bad idea. As beat up, as old as I am, nude doesn't work. Grabbed a shirt and undies, and she said,

"You're not in bad shape, you know."

"Thanks, I think."

Where was my hangover? I deserved a classic. Hadn't hit yet. Downstairs, I found her handbag, went through it. Tissues, lighter, lipstick, keys, condoms. Jeez, these girls travelled ready. Her wallet with ID revealed her to be Laura Nealon, twenty-eight, and she worked in phone sales. A fresh pack of Benson & Hedges; I tore them open, got one primed. Did the breakfast stuff. Found a tray, it had the wedding of Diane and Charlie. I even located serviettes. Shunted that up the stairs. She said,

"Oh, Jack, a picnic."

She patted the bed beside her. I declined and sat on the side. If she'd a hangover, it wasn't showing. Ate that toast with vigour, asked,

"May I use the shower?"

"Of course."

"Want to join me?"

"Ah, no, thanks."

"You're nice, Jack, I like you."

Hard for me to get a handle on all this good energy. Man, I'm so used to grief. It's familiar, almost comfortable. She returned, swathed in towels. I asked,

"Where did your friend go?"

"With Mr Keegan. She's crazy about him. We were so lucky to hook up with you guys."

I had to know, asked,

"Are you serious?"

"Completely. You wouldn't believe the animals out there. I'm going to hang on to you, Jack."

Then she was in my lap, doing things. Next thing, I'm having the blow job of my life. After, she asks,

"Was it good?"

"Brilliant."

"I'll make you happy, Jack, you'll see."

Heard the front door and thought,

"Oh, shit, Kiki's back."

Pulled my pants on and shuffled down. Sweeper was in the kitchen. I said,

"You're going to have to pack in this coming and going as you please."

"I rang the bell."

"Oh, I must have been in the shower."

Then he was looking behind me. I turned. Laura was there, in one of my shirts, said,

"Sorry, are my cigarettes here?"

Sweeper asked,

"Is this Kiki?"

"No . . . um, this is Laura."

"Hi."

"Hi."

I gave her the cigarettes, and she said,

"I better get ready, I'll be late for work."

When she'd gone upstairs, Sweeper asked,

"That's not your wife?"

"No."

"I see."

But he didn't and neither did I. I said,

"I've a definite lead."

"Tell me."

I did. He said,

"You're going to see this Bryson, I'll come with you."

"No."

We argued this for a while. Eventually he agreed and offered to give Laura a lift to work. I headed downtown. Went to the Vincent de Paul and bought a suit, sweater, shirts, jeans, blazer. Grand total: £35. The assistant said,

"Did you know each item is dry cleaned?"

"No, I didn't."

"The shops provide it free for us."

"Pretty good."

"It is."

Got a cab back to Hidden Valley with the gear. The driver said,

"Nice bit of clobber there."

"Dry cleaned, too."

"That'll do it."

I was a man with a new girlfriend, new wardrobe, the least I could provide was attitude. Wore the blazer with a crisp white shirt, grey slacks. I crackled in freshness. Coming outside, my neighbour said,

"You're like a new penny."

Heady praise.

The Simon is located at the top of the Fair Green. To the west is the train station, the coach depot to the south. Perhaps they like to hear the engines roar. Simon has saved countless lives from the Galway streets. It's clean, tidy, efficient and always available. In a city where most people have a bad word about most things, only Simon gets praise from all. I went in and a receptionist said,

"Howyah."

"Hello, I'm hoping to see Ronald Bryson."

"Hang on a sec."

There were no bad vibes. In a place that bears witness to such misery, you'd anticipate an air of depression. Not a hint. A tall lanky guy, over six feet two, in jeans, black T-shirt and suede waistcoat came ambling along. A ponytail and sharp acned features. An energy, like an Indian on the trail. No hurry, as he knew where you'd be. He drawled,

"I'm Ron."

I stood up, held out my hand, said,

"Jack Taylor. Appreciate you seeing me."

He waved a hand, ignoring my outstretched one, said,

"No sweat, Jack. Let's get some privacy."

English. That certain London inflexion of cool ease. I could dig if not grasp it.

He asked,

"Coffee?"

"No, I'm good, thanks."

We went into a small office. He went behind the desk, got comfortable in a chair and swung his legs up. Old battered moccasins, definitely bought in Nepal. I sat on a hard chair. He began to hand roll from a leather pouch, raised his eyebrows, an offer. I shook my head, got a red going. I leant over, gave him a light, he said,

"Nice lighter."

"Yes."

"Before we begin, Jack, let me tell you my position here. I'm not with the Community. I'm a trained social worker, fully qualified."

He paused and let me appreciate the full "weight" of this. I gave the appropriate half smile . . . too awed to speak. He resumed,

"So though I'm available to them, I'm not part of the organisation."

He stopped, so I said,

"Like a consultant."

Sour laugh.

"Hardly. Think of it more as an adviser."

"I have it now."

"Good, so what's your problem, Jack?"

I took out the list of travellers' names, laid it on the table, said,

"My problem is someone is killing the tinkers, these tinkers."

Legs swept off the table. All business now, he scanned the list and said,

"I know . . . knew these guys. I don't understand why it's your problem, Jack. You're not a guard and I'm sure you're not family."

Big grin here, to tell me he was a fun guy. That even though he'd terrific qualifications, he could banter with the guys. Like that. I said,

"I've been asked to check it out."

Note of incredulity in his voice, he said,

"Like a private eye, twenty a day and expenses? I love it; only in Ireland. I've seen the movies. Why'd you come to me, fellah?"

"You knew them."

"That's it! Wow, you're going to have to talk to a whole lot of people. They were tinkers. Man, they knew half the country."

"If there's anything . . ."

"Whoa . . . slow down, partner, and pad out those expenses. I want to see if I understand this correctly."

"What's to understand, Ron? Can you help . . . or not?"

"There's that gumshoe steel. Love it. No, what I'm trying to understand here is . . . have you any legal standing?"

"No."

"So, if I bounce you out of here like a bad cheque, you've got to bounce."

Ron was having a high old time.

"That's it, Ron. I'm appealing to your better nature."

Something crossed his face then. Not even a shadow, too fast, too insubstantial for that, but definitely from a dark neighbourhood. He said, teeth edged,

"You wouldn't want to make that mistake, Jack. I don't do appeals. That is not . . . never the way to conduct your dealings with me."

"Sorry, Ron, I guess I got carried away. I forgot you were a social worker."

The flicker again. I had no idea what button I was pressing, but it was jackpotting all over the place. I did, of course, know why I was doing it. To rattle the sanctimonious prick. Still edged, he said,

"You don't do well with authority, Jack. Let me see, you never had a real job, am I correct?"

This was more like it. This I could play, said,

"I was a guard."

Got him, but he rallied.

"Not to any degree of note, I'd say. Didn't burn up that ladder of success, did we?"

"You're very perceptive, Ron."

Preened, said,

"I've been doing this rather a long time, Jack."

"It shows. My trouble was they expected us to be social workers, too. Me, I had hoped to be human."

Didn't bite. The moment had passed, and Ron was back in mode. Gave me a full smile, said,

"I may have misread you, Jack. To be honest, I'd classed you as a wet brain. I've seen so many alkies, few are coherent."

"Hasn't dented your compassion though."

Nope, game over. He began the dismissal spiel, flicked the list with a nail.

"Those young men, all alkies. That life, it doesn't take many hostages. I'm a tad astonished you've survived so long yourself."

He stood up, added,

"Don't waste your time, Jack. They're just casualties of an indifferent war. It happens every day."

He put out his hand and I ignored it as he said,

"Leave your phone number. If something occurs to me, I'll call."

"Thanks, Ron. It's been educational."

"Not for me, Jack. In fact, it's been a shocking waste of my valuable time."

On the way out, I said to the receptionist,

"Thanks a lot. Ron was great."

"Everybody says that."

Outside, took a deep breath, shook off the creepiness whispering at my neck. Looked back. Pressed right against the window was Bryson. The panes distorted his features and gave the smile an eerie malevolence. His hand was at his groin, moving back and forth, mimicking masturbation. I only hope it was mimicry. What was I supposed to do? I did what any upright Irishman would do. I gave him the finger. Then I got the hell away from there.

"To do is to be."

Plato

"To be is to do."

Socrates

"Do be do be do."

Sinatra

I headed for The Quays. Keegan had said he'd be sussing out their lunchtime trade. He was. In full flow, telling an American couple that, yes, fields are still green in December. Then he sang the rest, truly hideous. He handed me a pint. I said,

"Jeez, that was fast."

"It's a fast country."

U2 were on the speakers—"Angel of Harlem". Keegan said,

"Fuck, how traditional is that?"

"To some, the most."

"But where's the diddley-do, all of them *bodhrans* and *uilleann* pipes?"

"Well pronounced."

"I've been practicing."

"It shows."

"Come on, Jack, is that hummable?"

"Well, of all the things you could say about U2, and George

Pelicanos has said most, I don't think hummable has been mentioned."

"Who's Pel . . . ican . . . os?"

"One of the best crime writers."

"Aw, shite talk; there's only Ed McBain."

He took a huge swallow of his pint, half in one swallow. Even the barman's jaw dropped. Keegan waited, then belched, said,

"My black pudding's near repeated."

"You ate that?"

"Oh, yea. Jury's give the full Irish job, including sausages, fried tomatoes, two eggs, bacon . . ."

"Rashers?"

"What?"

"In Ireland, we call bacon 'rashers'."

"Why?

"Because we want to."

"I was thinking of getting a tattoo."

"What?"

"With *Éire* and a shamrock, do you think?"

"Jeez, Keegan, it's hard to keep up with you."

"Drink up, that's my boy."

We got a table and he asked,

"How did you get on with that chick?"

"Come on . . . chick. Nobody calls them that except Terry Wogan."

"And?"

"It went good; it went brilliant."

"Me, too. I was riding half the night."

He spoke in a loud London boom so all the pub knew about the "ride". He looked like such a pig nobody challenged him. He asked,

"Didn't you go to see that social worker?"

"Bryson."

"The name sounds familiar."

"There is Bill Bryson the travel writer."

"I only read McBain. So how did it go?"

I ran it down. When I'd finished, he asked,

"What's your instinct?"

"He did them."

"Whoa, that's a jump, laddie."

"It's him."

"So now what?"

"I've got to find out all I can about him."

He took a pen out. To my amazement, it looked like a gold Parker. He said,

"It was a present from Unsworth."

"Unsworth?"

"A black woman cop, on my patch."

I was surprised, said,

"You're friends with a black person, with a black woman?"

He looked up, said,

"I have some moves. I'm not what I front . . . bit like you, Jack."

"I'll drink to that."

We did. I gave him all I knew about Bryson. He said,

"I'll get on the blower to my DI. If this monkey's a London boy, we'll dig him up."

"I appreciate it."

"Yea, so how come you're not getting the drinks in?"

Later he said,

"What's the plan in the immediate?"

"Soon as I find out where he lives, I'll go and burgle him."

"Count me in."

"You sure?"

"B and E is my speciality, OK? I'm going to get my tattoo . . . saw it on *Home and Away*."

"You watch that?"

"Doesn't everybody?"

In that moment, I don't know why, but I felt a surge of affection for him. He was standing there, like a fucked Popeye Doyle, sweating and heaving. Luckily he was gone before I said anything. The barman said,

"Jack."

"Yea."

"The Spice Girls have their ninth No. 1."

"Christ, why are you telling me?"

"Don't you like to stay informed?"

"Jesus."

The last time I saw the Spice Girls, I was coked to the far side of the moon. Posh looked uncannily like the young Cliff Richard. I still don't know which of them that's the worst news for; Beckam definitely.

When I got to Hidden Valley, I was in the bag. Finally took the clothes out of the dryer. They weren't so much dried as baked. The leather could stand up on its own, which was definitely the jump on me. I ironed it. They don't suggest, they bloody roar,

"Don't ever iron leather."

Fuck them.

The day before Cemetery Sunday, I finally went to visit my dead. Sweeper had lent me the van. He'd come early in the morning and asked me my plans for the day. I said,

"At Rahoon, those I have loved best and treated worst are lain. Over a year and I have not said Kaddish."

"Ka . . . what?"

"Respect."

He nodded solemnly; this he understood. If the clans comprehend one thing better than us, it's grief. God knows, they get enough practice. He asked,

"Do you wish me to keep you company?"

"No, I better do this alone."

"I will give you the van."

"Is it taxed?"

Big smile.

"Now, Jack Taylor, you sound like a guard. They say you were a fair one."

"I'll take the fifth on that."

The van was left in the lane within the hour. Chock-a-block with flowers. No more than Keegan, Sweeper had some moves. I wore the suit from Vincent de Paul. Fit fairish. In other words, you knew it hadn't been bought with me in mind. Sweeper had listened to my Bryson encounter, asked,

"You think it's him?"

"Yes."

"Then I'll kill him."

"Jeez, hold on. I have a few more checks to make."

"Then I'll kill him."

"Sweeper, for Christsakes, will you stop saying that. You asked me to help, you have to trust me."

"I trust you."

Begrudging.

"So no killing?"

"I'll wait."

"OK."

I drove the van up to Rahoon gates, took an armload of flowers. Two kids were kicking a ball just outside. One asked,

"Mister, you a tinker?"

"What do you care?"

"That's a tinker's van."

"How do you know?"

"No tax."

"Oh . . . should you be playing here?"

The second kid jerked a thumb at the dead, said,

"They don't care."

I levelled a look right at his eyes, asked,

"You sure?"

They left. First I said hello to my dad. I can say with my

hand on my heart that he was a real gentleman. In the old sense of that. A woman once told me,

"Your dad, he was gallant."

What a great word. He deserved it. Further on, I found Padraig's grave. The head wino for a brief glorious reign. He led his pack with flair and humour till he was run over by the Salthill bus. Some terrible irony in that, but it escapes me. I poured a small Jameson into the soil. That's a prayer he'd appreciate. Then Sean, the erstwhile owner of Grogan's. His delight in my once brief period of sobriety was too much to recall. He was murdered because of me. Guilt overload. I put roses there and I didn't say anything. While I was drinking, he wouldn't want to hear it. Nor could I possibly utter it.

The sheer bastardry of alcoholism. I wanted a drink so badly, I could taste it.

The fourth and final grave: Sarah Henderson. A teenage girl, her grave was immaculate, weeded, tidied and laden with framed poems and fluffy toys. Everyone from Britney through Barbie to a Barney doll. Her mother had come to me, pleading I prove her daughter was not a suicide. A number of young girls had died in an apparent "suicide epidemic". The case got solved. The girls had been murdered. The awful kicker was, Sarah did kill herself. Of course, I never told her mother. By then I was madly in love with her. I blew it all to hell and gone. A voice said,

"Jack."

For a moment, I thought Sarah had called. Then a shadow

fell across me. Ann Henderson, looking radiant. Her face glowing, those eyes looked at me. Summoning all my repartee, I said,

"Ann."

She looked at her daughter's grave, said,

"You brought six white roses."

"Well."

"You remembered, how wonderful."

I had no idea what to do. Tried to get my mind in gear, but
would it help? Would it fuck. She was examining me closely,
said,

"Your nose has been broken again. Oh, Jack, what are we
going to do with you?"

We!

She, however, could do whatever her heart desired. Am I
weak? Oh boy . . . and she was saying,

"But you have lovely teeth; are they crowns?"

"Mmm . . . sort of."

You'd think I'd have settled, got some bearings. No way,
José. She asked, in that awful concerned fashion exclusive to
those you've lost,

"How are you, Jack?"

I was giddy and, worse, reckless. Call it punch drunk. Said,

"I'm married actually."

Wouldn't that actually blow your head off? It did mine. I
prayed she wouldn't be happy for me. She gushed,

"Oh, Jack, how wonderful. Is she a local girl?"

"No . . . um . . . she's left me."

"Jack."

I had to know about her life, and even though I dreaded knowing, I asked,

"What about you, still seeing, um . . . ?"

"Yes, we've set a date for June. You'll have to come, promise you will."

I don't know what I said. I stumbled away, bumping into headstones, cursing, near weeping. On the side of the van, one of the kids had glow scratched,

"TINKER."

"And you have held my hand for reasons not at all."

I'd spoken on the phone with Laura. Went like this:

"Jack, I miss you."

"Good Lord, that's . . ."

"Will I see you?"

"Sure."

"Because Keegan is seeing my friend, like totally. She's going to try for his baby."

"That'll get his attention. Look, how about a meal tomorrow night?"

"You'll bring me to a restaurant, really?"

Why did I keep feeling she was winding me up? As soon as I got eager, people would leap out shouting,

"Ejit!"

Keep it low gear.

"I'll meet you at eight in Garavan's; we'll take it from there."

"I'll look really nice for you, Jack."

"I don't doubt it."

Had eased my way back from the daily intake of coke. This could only be a good thing. I went to bed early and seemed to only just have got to sleep when the phone rang. I checked the clock, four . . . went,

"This better be bloody vital."

"Jack, did I wake you?"

"Who's this?"

"Thought you'd be guzzling whiskey all night."

"Bryson."

"What happened to you calling me Ron? Ah, be friendly, Jack."

"Was there something?"

Could hear playfulness in his voice, a languid tone.

"I wanted to fuck with you, Jack, like you did with me today."

"You're getting there, pal."

"Been doing your homework on me, Jack?"

"Why . . . have you something to hide?"

"Am I like 'the Prime Suspect'? You, alas, are no Helen Mirren."

"Would you like that, Ron, being a suspect?"

"Don't patronise me, you worthless piece of sodden garbage."

"Whoa . . . got a hard on for drinkers . . . that it, Ron?"

"How dare you presume to analyse me. Think about this, Mr Private Dick . . . Ann Henderson."

I caught my breath. He heard it, said,

"Give you a start, did I, Jack? Now you have some clue as to who you're dealing with."

I needed some points fast; needed a cig, too, but fucked if I could see them, said,

"I know who I'm dealing with all right."

"Pray tell?"

This last in a falsetto.

"A sick fuck who jerks off against windows."

"8B, Hidden Valley, have I that right, Jack?"

Got me again, continued,

"Maybe I'll drop by, catch you unawares."

"You threatening me, Ron? I don't do threats well."

"You'll grow accustomed. Alas, I must grab some zzzzzs, an endless line of deadbeat drunks to fix tomorrow."

"Fix?"

"Oh, yes, Jack, I fix them fine. You'll see soon enough."

Click.

Got out of bed cursing,

"Where's the fucking cigarettes?"

I couldn't get hold of Keegan next day as he was touring Connemara. God help them, I thought. Sweeper was defending his position as leader of his clan. Literally. Every so often, a young buck would challenge and they'd settle it bare knuckled. Venues were usually held round Mullingar and attracted huge crowds. The betting aspect was the magnet, and fortunes were wagered. Nobody can generate cash flow like the clans. The guards would be reliably informed as to time, date and location. They'd overreact and flood a totally incorrect part of the country. The media particularly relished it and gave prime time to guards stopping innocent motorists. I had promised to attend at a later time. Not altogether sure I would.

I arranged to meet Brendan Flood. He suggested Supermac's. I got there first and took a table. Sign of the new Ireland, two black men were cleaning tables. I made a point of saying "Hello" but seemed to frighten them. Jesus, wait till they saw what the pubs and clubs disgorged at four in the morning. Then they'd know fear. Both the guards and the taxi men avoided it during the war zone. Those guys know. Brendan arrived in a suit, remarkably similar to my own recent purchase. I said,

"They get the dry cleaning free."

"Who?"

"Vincent de Paul."

"How do you know?"

"I'm a detective."

He looked round, and I asked,

"Why meet here?"

"They do lovely curried chips."

"Want some?"

"Oh, no. I gave them up for penance."

I let it slide. Would only open up all that ecclesiastical mayhem. I passed over a wad of money, said,

"For the missions."

"What do you need from me?"

"Ronald Bryson's address and the times he's out."

He nodded, asked,

"You met with him?"

"I did."

"Is he the one?"

"He's the one."

I took my mobile phone on the date. Rarely I took it anywhere.
I need to get out more. When it rings, it puts the shite cross-
ways in me, and I swear "never again". Only Jeff, Sweeper and
Keegan had the number. Gave me an artificial sense of control.
Dressed to impress. Wore the now-creaking leather. One day
of Galway rain would wipe them notions. A white shirt and
soft-to-softer faded jeans. You put them on, your body sways to
the music of thanks. The off-white colour between stone and
disintegration. Then the Bally boots. Oh, Kiki.

Walking down the town, two guards were coming towards
me. Their combined age might be twenty. I said in the Galway
vernacular,

"Min."

They said,

"Sir."

How old was that?

Garavan's was hopping nicely. Old Galway still prowls there. A school friend said,

"Jack."

I said,

"Liam."

No more. Irish warmth at its best; that is, completely understated. Works for me. Laura was sitting at the back, stood up to greet me. Wearing what can only be called a slip. It revealed everything. She did a twirl. I said,

"Wow!"

"It's a wow?"

"And more."

I wondered, if she sat, where would the dress go. She said,

"It's called a sheath."

"I'm not going to argue that."

I'd have said hankie, but there you go. She smelled great, so I told her. She said,

"It's Paris."

"It certainly is. What will you drink?"

"Metz."

I thought she was kidding, asked,

"Are you kidding?"

"No, I always have that."

"It's what the winos drink, 100 proof."

She was lost, said,

"It comes in a silver bottle, with schnapps and orange, says Metz in black letters."

"Oh."

Feeling a horse's ass, I went to the counter. Shelves of the stuff alongside all the other alcopops. Frigging evil it is. Came back with that and a pint, asked,

"Do you need a glass?"

"Oh, God, no."

In my youth, you drank from the bottle 'cause there were no glasses. The mobile went. I wasn't going to answer, but what if Sweeper was hurt? It was Jeff; he had hurt in his voice.

"Jack."

"Jeff, how's it going?"

"Cathy's had the baby."

"Oh, great. Is she OK?"

"I don't know. Could you come?"

"On my way."

Told Laura. She asked,

"Boy or girl?"

"Um . . ."

"What weight?"

"Um . . ."

"Jack."

"Jeez, Laura, these are women questions; guys never think to ask."

Leastways not any I knew.

She said,

"You better go."

"What about you?"

"Can I wait in Hidden Valley?"

"Course."

I gave her the keys. She spotted the miraculous medal, asked,
"Do you have a devotion to Our Lady?"

Irish women, they'll kill you every time. They juggle a mix
of blunt-nosed reality and a melting simplicity. Just when
you've them figured, they blow you away. I said, "Jeff gave it
to me."

"Then the baby will be fine."

She leant over, gave me a hard kiss, said,

"I'm up to me arse in love with you."

Like I said, blow you away.

The Time of Serena May.

I caught a cab at Dominic Street. He began,

"You know the trouble with Man U?"

As I got out at the hospital, he was saying,

"Know who I blame?"

Jeff was at reception, said,

"Let's go out, I need a smoke."

"But you quit."

"Jack . . . like I need a lecture from you?"

Fair enough. He looked awful. I've been wrecked so often, I'm surprised it's ever someone else. I didn't mention that. I shook loose the cigs, fired the Zippo, and he gulped down that smoke, said,

"If I'd coke, I'd demolish it."

In the time I'd known Jeff, he was Mr Cool. Never no fuss, no moods, just glided on by. Life had him by the balls now. I said,

"Do I say congratulations . . . buy cigars or what?"

"She had the baby."

"Boy or girl . . . oh . . . and what weight?"

"A girl. How would I know the weight? She's a tiny wee thing."

There! Right there was a difference. Jeff from *The Big Lebowski* was a father. All in a tone of voice. From hippie to protector in a few words. Truly astonishing. He was into it now.

"We've been here all day. Cathy, Jeez man, she's good as gold. Then six o'clock, said they'd do a section. I'm like sick, Jack. The nurse comes down, gives me her jewellery, I thought she'd died. Fuck, man, the whole world ended. Lose her and I'm totally gone."

For a moment he was, then snapped back.

"Ten to seven, they're going, 'Congratulations, you are a father,' but muted, man. I knew something was off. They show me this little bundle, and it's my daughter. I know nothing about babies, Jack, but she seems . . . limp. The paediatrician comes along, says, 'I am so sorry, your baby has Down's syndrome.'"

I think he's going to pass out.

"Jeff, yo buddy, can I get you something, tea, coffee . . . a drink?"

He takes another cig but not a light, goes,

"I can't get my head around it, is it cystic fibrosis, which flogging horror? I can get the names but not the details. Here's the tune, pal, but we can't help with the lyrics."

Long pause as he gasps for second breath, then,

"OK, the guy explains it. She has an extra chromosome;

she's mild, which means she'll take six months a year to catch up on other kids. I go down to Cathy, and you know what she says, Jack?"

I shook my head. Speak? . . . I couldn't even smoke.

"She says, 'Darling, I've let you down.' I'll carry those words to my grave. The nurse handed me the baby, and Cathy asks, 'Do you love her, love?' "

Then he physically dredged himself up, handed me the unlit cig, said,

"No, I won't be using them."

"Good man, you've got a daughter to raise."

They called her Serena May. Serena for the old Karmic vibe and May for "May all her dreams come true." Asked me to be the godfather. Jeff had invited me up to see the mother and daughter, and in that hospital room, I felt like an intruder. At first I demurred, saying,

"I'm not the godfather type."

Cathy gave me the look, so I added,

"I'd be privileged to be the guardian."

Jeff handed the baby to me and I made all the guy protests till Cathy said,

"Oh, go on, be a bad influence already."

Took her. This minute being, no more weight than half a pint, opens her eyes and looks. I said,

"She's eyeballing me."

Jeff said,

"She knows about 'the guards'."

I realised then for a fleeting moment what Thomas Merton

knew. Serena didn't have an extra chromosome; it was us, the normal ones, who were lacking the added spark. Would I could have held on to that moment, if I could have just sampled the energy for a little longer. I'd no longer need oblivion. Such knowledge is shocking, and few can handle it with care. I was even less able than I'd have imagined.

Back to Hidden Valley by four. The light in the kitchen. Laura was huddled in the armchair and immediately blurted out,

"He was here, he was waiting when I came in. I didn't see him at first and he gave me a terrible start. He seemed to think that was funny. He said he's a social worker who takes his work seriously and felt he should make a house call as you are drinking so much. He asked if I was your wife or if I was even Ann Henderson, and then he said that you, for an alcoholic, sure do manage to pull a lot of women and what was the attraction? Couldn't I find a normal guy or was this just some kind of weird kick?"

That she was now shaking uncontrollably tore my guts. I went over, bent down, said,

"It's OK now. I'm here and I won't leave you."

She grabbed hold of me, pulled me tight, said,

"He said he was a friend of yours, Jack."

"OK . . . did he touch you?"

"No."

"You sure?"

"Jack, he scared me."

"It's all right, honest; we'll go to bed and I'll hold you close, and nothing like this will ever happen again."

She believed me. As she drifted off to sleep, wrapped tight round me, I so badly wanted to go get the 9mm, go right round and blow his sick fucking head off. Those moments definitely influenced everything that subsequently happened. If I had to pinpoint one second when I made the worst judgement of my life, I'd say it began then.

Brendan Flood rang at noon the next day. Had the address and Bryson's work itinerary. I asked,

"How'd you get all this stuff?"

"The Lord provides."

"He sure does."

"I mentioned you at our group."

"Group?"

"We meet for prayers, say the rosary, ask for healing."

"I see."

Did I?

"Your name will be uttered for the next nine weeks."

Nine weeks, 9mm . . . ammunition of all kinds.

"Thanks, I think."

"Don't mock, Jack. Miracles happen; look at how I've repented."

That's what worried me. I rang Jury's and got a very groggy Keegan. I asked,

"Can we meet?"

"Oh, God, what time is it? What country is it?"

"Ireland."

"Shit, I thought I went home."

"Can you find the GBC at three?"

"Is it a pub?"

"It's a café."

"Not a pub?"

"We have work to do."

"Then it should be a pub."

And he hung up.

I considered bringing the gun, but wasn't Keegan as much weapon as anyone needs? He was late. I ordered a tea. The waitress said,

"We have lovely scones."

"So my mother says."

Her ears went back, interest riding high, asked,

"Do I know her?"

Time to shut her down, said,

"Hardly, she's dead."

No more pleasantries. When Keegan arrived, he got short shrift, and he said,

"That's the first unpleasant person I've met in Ireland."

"You think so? She offered me scones."

"Fuck her."

Despite this, he seemed remarkably chipper. I said so. He produced a silver hip flask. It had the Galway emblem. He said,

"My chick got it for me. It's got poteen."

"Poitín."

"Didn't I say that?"

"Sure you did."

He took a hefty slug, said,

"Argh . . . the waitress looks better already. Want a blast?"

"No, thanks. Bryson's been round my house."

I then relayed the events of the last few days, including Jeff's baby. He said,

"Down's syndrome. There was a villain on my patch, he had a little girl like that."

"How was she?"

He lit up.

"Chelsea, yea, I remember her name. Oh, she was a beauty, class act. Alas, I used her to hit at her old man."

"What?"

"Don't get pious on me, Jacko. I'm a cop, not a very nice guy, which is why we're here and I'm taking grief from some ugly cunt of a waitress."

He looked over at her. She'd been about to bring him a menu, but seeing his face, she changed her mind. He said,

"If a piece of filth like Bryson came to my house, put a fright on my woman, I'd put him in the ground."

He looked rabid. Spittle formed at the corner of his mouth. He continued,

"Last year, we'd a serial rapist in Clapham. The brass used my WPC as a decoy. Hung her out to dry, the reckless bastards. Her back-up got delayed. I didn't."

"What happened?"

"He had her on the ground, her tights torn off, a knife to her throat, shouting obscenities. I pulled him off, and know what he did?"

"No."

"He laughed at me, said he'd be out in six months and he'd do her then."

"Would he . . . be out?"

"Less time probably."

"So what did you do?"

"Helped him fall on his knife."

"What?"

"You heard me. Hadn't we better make a move?"

I said,

"Take a peek at the corner table by the door."

He did.

A well-dressed man, obviously distressed, was pouring out a story to a middle-aged couple. They were listening eagerly, hanging on to his every word. Keegan asked,

"What's going down, a scam?"

"If compassion is a scam, then yes. He's telling them in broken if well-accented English how he left a small bag in a café corner. But he is upset, so many cafés, they all seem alike. All his valuables are there, ticket, passport, credit cards."

"The mangy bastard, does he score?"

"He doesn't want anything, leastways nothing material. He gets off on their compassion, their joint upset at his calamity."

"You know him?"

"Sure, he used to be a guard."

"Someone should give him a slap round the earhole."

"Why? It's the much lauded 'victimless crime' in all its classic glory. All he takes is their time and a drop of their emotions."

We got outside and I said,

"Bryson has a studio apartment near the docks."

Keegan wasn't done with the compassion deal.

"This is one strange country, and you, Jack, might be the strangest in it."

"Ah, Keegan, come on, don't tell me you don't have characters like him on your beat?"

"Dozens. In London, though, he'd get their address, then come some slow Tuesday, he'd nip round, rape the woman, behead the man."

"That happened?"

"I had a dog once, Meyer Meyer, after a character in Ed McBain, a mongrel. I heard they can be babe magnets."

"Was he?"

"He got the babes, all right. I got the dogs, still barking some of them."

I laughed.

"There was a psycho loose then, the papers called him 'the Torch'. He covered Meyer in petrol, flicked a match."

"Jesus."

"I liked old Meyer, he was good company."

"What did you do to the Torch?"

"Nothing."

"Ah, come on, Keegan."

"We never caught him."

"Oh."

"Each broken truth I've sold, I've understated."

Phyl Kennedy

Christopher McQuarrie, The Usual Suspects screenwriter, turned director with *The Way of the Gun,* said,

"I was afraid of hiring James Caan because I'd heard stories. Then the first thing he said to me was, 'You sick fuck.'

"I guess he'd heard stories about me, too."

I was telling Keegan this as we approached Merchants Road, but a trawler away from the docks. I asked him,

"How do we play this?"

He gave a sardonic smile, said,

"Straight."

He produced keys and got us through the front door. Up one flight to 107, the apartment. Keegan again with the keys and we were in. The first sensation was smell, reek of incense. Keegan said,

"Our boy likes to smoke dope."

"He smokes incense?"

"Cop on."

I tried.

A large living room, looking like a garbage tip. Throw rugs on the floor, items of clothing scattered everywhere. Keegan said,

"Not a tidy lad."

The kitchen was a mess. Discarded cartons of junk food on every surface. Dishes piled high on the sink. Keegan ordered,

"You do the living room, I'll toss the bedroom."

I found a stack of *Time Out's,* the gay listings particularly well-thumbed. On the table was Fred Kaplan's *Gore Vidal.* I shouted that in to Keegan and added,

"Shit, it's signed."

"By Fred or Gore?"

I was impressed by the question. He came out of the bedroom with a stack of mags, said,

"Hard-core S and M, gay, fetish and the perennial favourite, pain."

"Not proof though, is it?"

"Proof's overrated."

"Not in court."

"That's what you think. Do you never watch *The Practice*?"

We rummaged some more but found nothing further. As we left, I put the Vidal book in my pocket. Keegan said,

"He's going to miss that."

"I know."

"And the half weight of grass?"

"You took the dope?"

"Or vice versa."

That evening, I was stocking the bookshelf. I'd been on another visit to Charlie Byrne's and come away laden. I wasn't anal retentive, didn't need those volumes alphabetically or in neat alignment. No, I liked to stir it. Put Paul Theroux beside St Vida. That was wicked. Line Pellicanos with Jim Thompson, Flann O'Brien with Thomas Merton. Over the past six months, I'd read *House of Leaves, Heartbreaking Work of Staggering Genius* and discovered David Peace.

To hand was Anne Sexton's poems *To Bedlam and Partways Back*. Another writer whose suicide and life of derangement threw shadows of dark identification. The doorbell went. Sweeper nearly fell in the door. His eye was blackened, bruising on his face, suit torn and blood on his hair. He limped to a chair, said,

"A whiskey please, Jack Taylor."

I made it large. He gulped it down and I gave him a cigarette. I said,

"You fought in your suit?"

"This was not a challenge."

"Something else, was it?"

"Something else, you might say that."

He fixed those dark eyes on me, asked,

"How do you feel about us tinkers?"

"You have to ask?"

"Today . . . yes."

"I'm working with you and glad to do so."

Those eyes unwavering.

"And if we lived next door, Jack Taylor, how would that be?"

"Lively."

Gave a short smile.

"Let's see how true that is."

"You don't believe me?"

"Come on."

The van was parked in the alley, huge dents on its surface. I
asked,

"Jeez, what happened, people hurl rocks or something?"

"Exactly."

He put the van in gear, asked,

"You know what a halting site is?"

"Where they place the clans, like a camping ground."

That amused him. He muttered,

"Camping ground, how ordinary that sounds."

The stench of condescension leaked from the words. I said,

"Hey, Sweeper, ease up with the tone. Whatever happened, I'm not part of it. I'm with you, remember?"

A bitterness worked its way down from his eyes to his mouth, caused a tic to vibrate above his lips. He scratched at it, said,

"You're from the settled community. No matter how outlaw you think you are, you're part of them."

I let it go but I didn't fucking like it. Shook out a cig. Sweeper ordered,

"Light two."

The child in me wanted to roar,

"Buy your own."

I lit them, handed one over. He said,

"I've offended you, Jack Taylor."

"Don't sweat it, pal."

He concentrated on his driving. The nicotine joined the cloud of tension. He pulled up at Dangan Heights and we got out. He nodded towards the valley, said,

"Look."

Mainly I could see smoke. I said,

"Fires, bush fires. So what?"

"That's the . . . camping ground."

Focusing, I could see people, wandering stunned through the haze. Men, limping, were vainly ferrying water in a futile effort to douse the flames. Children, barefoot, were crying, clinging to mothers. Not a caravan was untouched. Those not aflame were overturned or charred. I asked,

"Where are the guards?"

He snorted with derision, asked,

"You listen to the news, right?"

"Sure."

"Did you hear anything about this?"

"No."

"Because it's not news."

"Who did it?"

"The upright citizens you'll find in church."

I thought of my mother, didn't argue. I looked at his hair, his clothes, said,

"You were there."

"Yes, but I arrived late. Not that it made any difference. I did stop two from castrating one of my cousins."

"It sounds like *Soldier Blue*."

"It sounds like Ireland today."

"What will you do now?"

"Rebuild. It's what we always do."

"I don't know what to say."

He clapped my arm, said,

"Come on, I'll drive you back."

"Could I go down, help somehow?"

"A settled person would not be welcome today or for many days."

We drove back in silence. At the house, I said,

"Call me if you need anything."

"I need one thing, Jack Taylor."

"Name it."

"Find whoever's killing my people."

*"What laws shall you fear if you dance
but stumble against no man's iron chains?"*

Khalil Gibran, *The Prophet*

*

I had no idea how to get Ronald Bryson. Shooting him was the most attractive idea. Proof, some bloody proof. I could pray, of course, but held little store in that. Whatever else, I didn't think faith would nail the bastard. So I did what I do when I'm stuck. I read. Call it escape, I call it calm. My most recent find was Robert Irwin. A joy to my heart, a Cambridge scholar and wild drug user. Him I'd have liked on a pub crawl. How could it miss? His brilliant crazy work, *Satan Wants Me,* had just been reissued. Set in swinging London in 1967, it's beyond definition. So taken was I, I had got Vinny to track down *An Exquisite Corpse,* about surrealism in 1930. They don't have to be read in the west of Ireland with a line of coke and a large tumbler of Black Bush, but Christ, it sure enriches the rush.

My strategy on finishing those was to revisit James Sallis. In particular, his Lew Griffin novels, and then I'd be in the perfect zone for embracing mayhem. The phone went. I gulped some Bush and picked it up.

"Jack!"

"Laura?"

She was weeping, gasping for breath. I said,

"Take it slow, hon, I'm here. Just tell me where you are."

"In a phone booth on Eyre Square."

"Don't move, I'll be right there."

I found the kiosk and a near hysterical Laura. When I opened the door, she jumped. I said,

"It's OK . . . shhss."

I cradled her, and a woman passing glared at me, her eyes shooting venom. I said,

"I didn't do it."

"That's what they all say."

Laura pushed a crushed package to me. The Zhivago logo. She said,

"I got you a present, Jack."

That nearly killed me. Put that feeling on top of rage and you're holding high explosive. I got Laura to a bench. A wino was slumped at one end, humming softly. Sounded like a Britney Spears tune.

Go figure.

I asked,

"What happened, darling?"

"I was talking to Declan in Zhivago and I saw that man."

"Which man?"

As if I couldn't guess. She said,

"The English fellah who came to your house."

"Bryson."

"He followed me out of the shop."

"You should have told Declan, he'd have put his shoe in his hole."

"I didn't want to make a fuss."

And so evil flourishes and spreads because decent people don't want to make a fuss. She continued,

"He spooked me. I'd got as far as Faller's when he caught up. He said, 'Don't be in such a hurry. I'm not going to hurt you. I'd like you to deliver something to our Jack, could you do that?'

"I said I would and he spat in my face."

I wiped her face as if the spittle was still there. I felt near blind from fury. Lifted her up, said,

"I'm going to bring you to some friends of mine, OK?"

She clung to me, pleaded,

"So you won't let him hurt me, Jack?"

"I guarantee it, sweetheart."

I got her to Nestor's. Jeff was tending bar, the sentry in his usual slot. I put Laura in the hard chair, walked to the counter. The sentry asked,

"Have you another wife?"

I said to Jeff,

"This girl has had a shock; would you mind her for a bit?"

He raised an eyebrow but said,

"I'll get Cathy."

"How's Serena May?"

"Doing good."

"I'll be back in a few minutes."

The madness was burning. I'd have anybody.

Jeff said,

"Don't do anything crazy."

"What's that mean?"

He raised his hands in mock surrender, said,

"Hey, back off, buddy. You should see your face."

I left.

Tearing along Forster Street. I heard my name called. Ignored it, kept going. Felt my arm grabbed. Whirled round to face Keegan. He said,

"Slow down, boyo."

"Fuck off."

He didn't let go of my arm, said,

"It's been a long time since anyone said that to me, Jack."

"You want to let go of my arm?"

"Tell me what you're doing, Jack."

I gave a long sigh, one my mother would have been proud of. Could feel some of the white heat dissipating. I wanted to hug it closer, said,

"I'm going to tear that fucker's head off."

"Not smart, Jack."

"Screw smart. You said yourself you'd destroy anyone who touched your woman."

He nodded.

"But not with witnesses. Let me go up there, see what the story is. You hang here, smoke a cig, get your act together."

It made sense, so I said,

"It makes sense."

"OK, see you anon."

I watched him walk to the green, turn towards the Simon. Even from a distance, you could sense the balled up menace of his posture. I tried not to think about the damage I wanted to inflict. Sat on the small wall, favoured seat of many drinking schools. The meths passed round here didn't come in a fancy bottle or get stocked in trendy pubs. No, it was true rot gut, what they called "Jack" or "White Lady" in south-east London, 100 proof methylated spirits. I'd sipped it on rare occasions.

Moved my mind to books. Tommy Kennedy had said,

"There'll be times when the only refuge is books. Then you'll read as if you meant it, as if your life depended on it."

My life and certainly my sanity had fled to reading through a thousand dark days. Resolved to get hold of James Sallis and his bio of Chester Himes. I'd reread all of David Gates. His *Jernigan* was my life if I'd had a formal education. Heard,

"Jack!"

Snapped out of it, looked at Keegan. He asked,

"Jeez, Jack, where did you go?"

"I was here."

"Not if your eyes are any guide. Tell you, boyo, you're going to have to quit the nose candy; it's frying your brain."

"I was thinking of books."

"I rest my case."

I stood up, asked,

"What went down?"

"He's legged it, gave his notice."

"Fuck."

Connections were screaming in my head, couldn't match them. Keegan said,

"My govenor came through from London."

"Who?"

"My chief inspector."

"What did he find out?"

"Our boy comes from money, like major bucks. Did public school, all that good shit. He's a bona fide social worker all right. Now here's the thing, he was attached to at least ten centres. The ones who had either street alcoholics or what the do-gooders call 'the Marginalised'. He always left each place under a cloud. No specific charges, but a definite cloud of disturbance. So, people could disappear, who the fuck would notice? Then he did what the smart sickos do; he emigrated."

The connection hit. I said,

"He follows Laura, deliberately, assaults her, knowing what she'll do. That she'll call me. I'll come charging and my house is empty."

Keegan nodded, said,

"Let's get down there."

"He'll have been and gone."

"But let's see what he's gone and left you."

On our way there, he said,

"You think, Jack, that I don't get the Irish. That I'm some sort of plastic paddy."

I started to protest but he ploughed on.

"Just because I love the blarney shit doesn't mean I'm blind. My mother was Irish, and when they're rearing kids in England, they're more Irish than you'll ever know. She used to say, 'Rear? I didn't rear ye, ye were kept at room temperature like Fruitfield jam.' You might have lived here, laddie, but I was fucking marinated in it. I knew what a hurley was before I could walk. When she used it, I definitely couldn't walk. So do me a favour, pal, don't pull Celtic rank on me."

I was saved from a reply as we'd arrived at the house. The door was open. Keegan went,

"Uh-oh."

And went first. The smell hit straight away. A huge crap in the kitchen. All the crockery was smashed and excrement smeared on the walls. In the front room, the new books were in tatters, the remains piled on the slashed sofa and reeking of urine. Keegan said,

"I'll get cleaning."

I went upstairs. My new clothes in bits and stuffed in the toilet, a note left on my pillow.

"Wanna play, Jack?"

Keegan shouted,

"Bad?"

The coke was gone, but more worrying, so was the 9mm. I

was debating whether to tell Keegan when the phone rang. He said,

"I'll get it."

Obviously I only got Keegan's side, which went like this.

"Jack's not available. Oh, I know who you are, Ronald. Who am I? I'm Detective Sergeant Keegan from the Met, and I've a full report on you, son. Quite a work record. Oh dear, that's very foul language. Yes, I've seen your actions here. Very impressive. I do hope you wiped your arse. Don't shout, Ron, that's a good lad. You're leaving the country! Think about this, boyo; some day soon, you'll get a tap on the shoulder and guess who? We have something in common . . . Oh, yes, I have a very dodgy past. I'm the animal you *Guardian* readers get orgasms about. No, no, Ronald, don't worry about jurisdiction, because I certainly won't. You'll get to shit your pants again, and I'll make you eat it. Okey-dokey, cheerio . . . lovely to chat with you."

I was standing next to Keegan as he hung up, asked,

"He's leaving?"

"So he says."

"I had a gun here; it's gone."

"No sweat, I'll make him eat that, too."

"I don't think he'll go yet."

"Me neither."

Keegan said he'd yellow-page it and have the house cleaned, told me,

"Go see your girl."

"Thanks, Keegan."

"It's no big deal. It's what I do, clean up shite."

"I feel odd calling you Keegan all the time. What's your first name?"

"You feel odd! Gee, that's a pity, get over it."

*"All islanders, no matter what their ethnicity, live with a certain kind of longing.
It's a type of travel that is kept in check by fear of the unknown world.
White people just make an aesthetic out of it. Living on an island
is its own excuse to stay home and dream."*

John Straley, *The Angels Will Not Care*

AT ROCHES, THEY WERE SELLING BADGES. I'D ALMOST PASSED WHEN
the name struck me; pushed a note in the box, took two
badges. Put one in my lapel and the other in my pocket. When
I got to Nestor's, Jeff was watching Sky News, said,

"Another recount, but I think Bush will get it. That or jail."

The sentry asked,

"Is McGovern still alive?"

No one answered, so he added,

"I liked Carter because of the peanuts."

Jeff said,

"The girl is fine. She's upstairs with Cathy and the baby."

He caught the glint of gold in my lapel, asked,

"What's with the badge? Not the Pioneers, is it?"

I moved close, let him have a good look. It was two hands,
the fingers barely touching. He asked,

"What's it in aid of?"

I took a deep breath, aware that this could go horribly wrong, said,

"The Down's Syndrome Association. Represents ordinary society reaching out to . . ."

I stopped, had put it across in the worst way. He said,

"I like it."

I took the second from my pocket, said,

"Here."

He held it in his hand, said,

"You took a risk."

"You know me, Jeff, Mr Sail-Close-to-the-Wind."

He pinned it on his shirt, said,

" 'Preciate it."

Upstairs everybody was hugging the baby. Cathy was watching with a wondrous expression. I asked,

"Everybody's doing OK?"

Cathy smiled, said,

"Never better."

Spent the afternoon there. I managed some slow pints, nothing major. I'd have crawled into a bottle of whiskey, but they'd have murdered me. So, took it easy. Cathy made stew that tasted terrific. Laura asked,

"How did you learn this, you're English?"

"Well, I put everything in, heavy with the meat and potatoes, then I almost overcooked it, and Jeff said . . . add *poitín*."

She pronounced it like a woman from Connemara. In my life of turmoil, it is so rare for me to be part of a domestic scene. Not that I didn't want it. I did, but I wasn't prepared for the small acts of devotion that lead up to it. My nature is essentially selfish, and to participate in family life you have to make room for others. Too, I'd mastered the art of sabotage. To paraphrase Oscar, each alcoholic destroys the image he craves. I wanted to be able to get drunk when I wanted and read till dawn if I wanted and wasn't able to make the jump to forgo such things for the sake of company. And yet, how I yearned to be different. To sit in the warmth of family and just be easy. But that day, I was lucky. I knew how much I appreciated the moment. Thank God, I didn't have to wait for the verdict of hindsight. The storms, ever present on my chart, seemed less threatening. As we were leaving, Cathy, unwittingly, verbalised the death knell, said,

"We should do this more often."

I knew, sure as shooting, we never would. The awareness blunted but didn't erase the glow. Laura linked my arm as we walked to Hidden Valley. She asked,

"Did you like the CD?"

Jesus, I'd completely forgotten her pushing the packet into my hand. I'd stuffed it in my jacket and never given it another thought. I said,

"I didn't want to open it till we were together."

"Oh, you're so romantic, Jack."

Yeah, right. I warned,

"The house is in a state."

"Was it . . . him?"

"No, it was yahoos."

The house was spotless Not a sign of the chaos. Even the

bookshelf was stocked, even if it seemed to be all of McBain's eighty publications. I said,

"Wow!"

"Jack, the house looks great."

"Sure does."

I couldn't believe Keegan had restocked the bookcase. That impressed the hell out of me. I'd check the titles later. Joy is so random, you have to ration it carefully. I said,

"Let's have a drink."

"Let's go to bed."

"Let's do both."

We did.

It was good. No doubt, I was improving. I'd never be a hot gasp lover, but I was definitely focusing. What I lacked in expertise, I was compensating with energy. Lying in bed, I opened the Zhivago bag, looked at the CD, went,

"Oh, my God."

She sat up alarmed,

"You don't like it?"

It was *Just Another Town* by Johnny Duhan. I said,

"I love it, but it opens a box of memories I don't know am I able for."

Back in '82, I was still in uniform, dating a girl from Boher-more. Man, I played that album to death. A track, "Shot Down", was the very breath I inhaled. The girl would say,

"Are we having a Johnny Duhan day?"

Were we ever? And more than any decent person could bear. Over the dark years, I'd keep pace with each Johnny album. As his songs deepened, I spiralled ever down. Before the girl dumped me, she said,

"Don't get me wrong, Jack, I like sad songs, but you . . . you need them."

I knew she was right. There has never been an occasion when, if I encountered a brass band, I didn't want to weep. Freud that. Later, when the CD was playing—I mean later, as in weeks on—and Sweeper was in the kitchen and "Just Another Town" was playing, he said,

"That's the first time I ever heard my upbringing in a song."

I gave him the thing, what else could I do? In the terrible months of soul darkness when these events had concluded, I went and rebought the whole Duhan catalogue. Only Emmylou Harris reaches me thus.

Back to the moment with Laura, I shook my head as if that would erase the memories, said to her,

"You couldn't have got me anything better."

"I was going to buy Elvis. Do you like him?"

"Hon, I judge people on whether they like him or not."

She gave the most radiant smile. Times are now, I wish I'd never experienced her happiness. The pit opens and I rush headlong. She said,

"I wrote you a poem."

I didn't know how to respond, went for,

"You write?"

Trying to keep the astonishment from my voice. Shaking her head, she said,

"Oh, God, no; just this one."

She reached over to her bag, took out a pink sheet of paper, handed it over solemnly. I opened it with a stone heart, mantra-ing,

"No, this will not touch me in any way."

Read:

> *The love that hurts.*
> *By*
> *Laura Nealon, Galway, Ireland.*

That first piece had me full fucked and I still had the poem looming. Focused.

> *My love I have lost*
> *The love from the west*
> *I long for the night*
> *The night that will come*
>
> *Upon my pillow I will lie*
> *My love beside*
> *I long to touch*
> *The love to watch*
>
> *At your side*
> *I love to breathe*
> *I love to kill*
> *By my love's side*
> *I wish to lie.*

I don't know much, but I knew I was going to need strong drink soon and a whole shipful. I said,

"It's terrific."

"I won't write any more, it was just to . . ."

"Thanks a lot."

After a while, she asked,

"Was your wife very smart?"

"She left me, how smart can you get?"

She let that dance, said,

"Cathy said she went to college."

Cathy had a big mouth. I said,

"Yes."

"To do what?"

Jeez, on top of the poem, I was perilously close to bluntness, said,

"A doctorate in metaphysics."

She bit her lower lip, said,

"I don't know what that means."

I relented, said,

"Hon, the places I've been, the places I'm likely to be, it wouldn't buy you a dry spit."

She mulled that over, then,

"I'm not sure what that means either, but it makes me feel better."

Sleep was creeping up on me. I said,

"Get some rest, hon."

"OK, but in my job I make tons of money. I'll give you some."

Jesus!

She was gone early next morning. I had what they call an emotional hangover. Would settle for the booze variety any day. Leastways, you knew how to deal with it. An envelope had been pushed through the door. Opened it cautiously: a wedge, whole stack of large denomination. A note:

You'll be short, don't be.

Sweeper.

His handwriting was superb. Almost as if he'd used a quill; shit, maybe he had.

One of the first lessons you learn as a guard is hard men. They don't teach this in the manual. You learn it on the streets. Every town has its quota. They are hard in the true sense. Ruthless, unyielding, merciless. Unlike the pub version, they don't advertise their mettle. There's no need. It's in the eyes. The ones I'd encountered all shared one trait: a granite fairness. Never mind that it was their take on it, they stuck by it. Bill Cassell. Isn't that a hell of a name? Nobody, and I emphasise nobody, ever cracked wise about the dictionary. He was a hybrid, a Galway mother and a father from hell. Bill had a fearsome reputation. The guards kept their distance. I'd gone to school with him. For years, he'd taken numerous beatings till he grew, and then he dished them out. Every teacher who'd ever thrashed him got a reprisal. Later, rather than sooner. He was a man of infinite patience.

There's a pub on the docks called Sweeney's, small, dark and dangerous. A chance dropper-in gets carried out. Tourists do not find it. I planned on a visit. Went to Dunnes and splashed out. Big time. I'd shopped in charity outlets for so long, I was truly appalled at real prices. But said fuckit; I had a stash. Shot through the shop like a mini Haughey. Balls, attitude and dubious taste. Four sweatshirts, three jeans, permacrease chinos, sneakers, white Ts, sports jacket. The assistant asked,

"Have you got a club card?"

"Take a wild guess."

"I'm supposed to ask."

I had no idea why I was giving her grief. You work for Dunnes, you have shovelfuls already. I handed over a small ransom, read her name tag, said,

"You're doing a great job, Fiona."

"How would you know?"

"*Touché*. You'll go far."

Brought the stuff home. Considered: for a villain meet, did you dress up . . . or down? Compromised. New navy sweatshirt, faded jeans and a fucked leather. Now if that wasn't a mixed message, then my time in the guards was truly wasted. Transferred the Down's syndrome pin to the leather. I looked like that wanker who advertises insurance for the over fifties. Had a quick listen to Johhny Duhan and I was set. Walking down Shop Street. I saw my mother looking in Taffes' window. There was nothing in it, not a single item. I kept walking. At Griffin's bakery, I met the bookie I had once fleeced. The aroma of fresh bread was like hope. I said,

"How's it going?"

He indicated his bread, said,

"I got my grinder."

"That'll do it."

"You won't be calling any time soon?"

"I hadn't planned to."

"Good news at last."

A refugee asked me for my jacket. I said,

"It's got sentimental value."

"I don't care, give it to me."

Jesus.

The docks are full changed. When I was a child, it was a magical if forbidding zone. Equal part danger and temptation. Dockers were men of true stature. You might fuck with all types but never them. I was lucky to have met the very best of them. Luxury apartments, new hotels, language schools and leisure craft had overtaken the area. It might have been progress, but it was not an improvement. An oasis of old Galway was Sweeney's. I think developers were too intimidated to approach the owners. I pushed open the door, inhaled the mix of fish and nicotine. Conversation died till they got a fix on me. Then, an audible sigh of ease and talk resumed. Bill had a table near the bar. He was alone.

For a man of fearsome reputation, he had a slight frame. Slighter now. The skin on his face seemed stretched to burst. As if someone had applied an undercoat, then forgot to add the finish. His eyes, still granite, were deep set in his skull. A glass of fresh orange juice in an old style glass stood before him. Pips floated near the surface. He said,

"Jack."

"Bill."

"Take a seat."

I did.

Up close and personal, he looked like an Aids victim. He said, without moving, to the barman, "Pint for Jack."

I asked,

"Can I smoke?"

He gave a dry smile, said,

"Course."

The ashtray was advertising Capstan Mild. I shook loose a red, fired up with the Zippo. Bill put out a skeletal hand, asked,

"Mind if I have a look?"

I passed it over. He hefted it in his palm, said,

"Bit o' weight."

"Yes."

"Want to sell it?"

"It's on loan."

"Isn't everything?"

The pint came. Probably among the better poured. I said,

"*Sláinte.*"

For one awful second I'd nearly said,

"Good health."

Bill let me savour the moment, then,

"What do you want, Jack?"

"Help."

He stared at his orange juice before saying,

"I heard you did a number on the Tiernans."

"Not friends of yours, I hope?"

"If they were, you wouldn't be sitting there."

The barman leaned over, said,

"You're wanted on the phone."

"Not now."

Then back to me.

"You're running around town with a cop."

"I am."

"Jesus, Jack, an English one."

"He's part Irish."

"Bollocks."

The word shook his delicate body. I asked,

"Are you sick?"

"Liver cancer."

"Oh, God."

"I don't think God had a lot to do with it. Blame Sellafield, least it's English. What kind of help had you in mind, Jack?"

"There's a girl, named Laura Nealon."

"I know the family."

"I want her protected."

"Who's after her besides yourself?"

"An English guy, name of Ronald Bryson, works sometimes with the Simon."

Bill was shaking his head.

"What is it with you and the English? You spent years planning to go to London, all the time, London's coming to you."

"You have a point."

"OK, Jack, you know how this works or you wouldn't have come. I'll arrange what you ask. But I don't need to remind you, there's no free lunch."

"Meaning I owe you."

"Exactly."

"What do you want?"

"Who knows? You'll get a call asking for a favour. It's not negotiable."

"I know how it works."

"Be sure you do, Jack."

The interview was over. I stood up, asked,

"How's your mother?"

"Dead, thanks."

In 1987, a garda training committee, its report on probationer training, defined for the first time a philosophy for the modern garda. The citizen expected police officers:

To have the wisdom of Solomon, the courage of David, the strength of Samson, the patience of Job, the leadership of Moses, the kindness of the good Samaritan, the strategical training of Alexander, the faith of Daniel, the diplomacy of Lincoln, the tolerance of the carpenter of Nazareth and finally an intimate knowledge of every branch of the natural, biographical and social sciences.

If he had all these, he might be a good policeman.

Parts of that had swirled through my dreams, and I slept till noon the following day. I was deep whacked. All the events of the preceding days had found voice and cried,

"Enough."

I'd left messages for Keegan, Laura, Sweeper. To Keegan to say, "Thanks." To Laura to say, "Let's go dancing." To Sweeper to say, "Nearly there." The three messages contained only two lies. Cokeless, I'd got into bed with a hot toddy and one of the books furnished by Keegan. *Kiss Tomorrow Goodbye* by Horace McCoy, a classic of *noir*, though McCoy was best known for *They Shoot Horses, Don't They?* Halfway through the drink I was asleep. At least all I was burning was a bulb.

I took a long shower, blasted away the cobwebs. A glance in the mirror. Time to trim my beard, managed it without a tremor, progress of the slanted variety. Fresh sweatshirt, new jeans, and I was cooking. Downstairs to an envelope. Recognised the handwriting: Kiki. A bit of weight so it was going to be comprehensive; coffee first. I was feeling good not stupid. Two slices of toast with sizzling strips of bacon. Or rashers, as I'd told Keegan. Put that away, poured second coffee, lit a red and breathed Kiki. Opened the letter.

Dear Jack

The term metaphysics does not always evoke the same idea in different minds. In some people, it gives rise to a feeling of aversion because for them it means vague speculations, uncontrollable assertions and a trespassing of the boundaries of reason which is more akin to poetry than talking. Others see just the opposite in metaphysics, namely an extraordinarily obstinate effort to think clearly and cogently. Would it help you, Jack, to know the origin of the term? Among Aristotle's works there are a few short treatises concerned with what he calls first philosophy. These were united into a work of ten books, which, as is supposed, Andronicus of Rhodes in his edition of Aristotle's works called La Meta Physic, because of their location after the physical treatises.

Is this clear to you, Jack?

Do be clear on this, I'm divorcing you.

Kiki

On the radio, Seamus Heaney is saying Ireland is chic. Keegan would agree, though his description might be a little more colourful.

I got a new case!

I was having a coffee in Nestor's when a man approached.

"Mr Taylor, might I have a moment?"

"Sure, and it's Jack."

Another English accent. I hoped Bill didn't get wind of it. He was about my age, with the air of an accountant, a heavily receding hairline and a face that just missed being interesting. He was dressed in jeans, and a heavy denim jacket. Said,

"I'm Michael Tate. Perhaps you've heard of me?"

"No."

"Or the GSF?"

"Nope."

He seemed very put out, so I said,

"Tell me what it means?"

"The Galway Swan Foundation."

"Oh."

"It's purely voluntary. We take care of the swans."

"Great."

"Have you been reading the *Galway Advertiser*?"

"Not attentively, no."

"Someone is decapitating the swans."

"Jesus."

"The guards haven't the time to mount an investigation. We heard you get results."

"I don't know. I . . ."

"Seven swans in two weeks. We will pay you, of course."

"Where does it happen and when?"

"The early hours of the morning, in the Claddagh Basin."

"Why don't you rally your members, mount a continuous watch."

He looked down at his shoes. A pair of brown brogues from Dunnes. I'd considered the very pair on my recent expedition. He said,

"The majority of our members are not in the first flush of youth, Mr Taylor. Even if we did as you suggest, the person who's doing this . . . well, we'd be no match for such an individual . . . or worse, a gang."

"When was the last attack?"

"A week ago. It's usually a week between them."

"OK, I'll give it a go."

He stood up, gave me an envelope.

"I hope this will be sufficent."

After he'd gone, I opened the envelope. A single twenty pound note. I wanted to shout,

"The drinks are on me."

I didn't get to investigate that night. I'd halfways planned on buying some thermal gear, going down to the Claddagh in the early hours of the morning, but it got away from me. Laura had to cancel our evening, asking,

"Jack, can we please go dancing another time?"

"Sure."

In John Straley's book is the following:

In my universe there are drinkers and dancers. And the two should never intermingle. I have always been with the drinkers, self-conscious introverts who crack wise about the music and sneer at the dancers at the same time. They are consumed with envy.

The plan as usual was at fault. This was the plan: I'd go to a quiet pub, have one quiet drink and go quietly home. Yeah. Of late, my hangovers had been manageable. Just a slight nausea and the fragile feeling. Now, the reckoning had come with ferocity. Came to on the floor of my kitchen, half a green chicken on the table. Threw up there and then, then crawled through the morning. Whatever I attempted—tea, toast, water—just up-chucked. I was not a well person. A measure of how bad, a song kept repeating in my head. "Bend It" by Dave Dee, Dozy, Beaky, Mick and Tich. I could recall them on *Top of the Pops* in the sixties with Davy lashing a bullwhip: could hear the whistle of the rawhide even now.

Headed for Nestor's and, thankfully, I met nobody. I

couldn't hold a match, never mind a conversation. Jeff was stocking up. I asked,

"Before you start, tell me, was I here last night?"

He shook his head and I said,

"That means what exactly?"

"You're going down the toilet, Jack."

I could lay into him, but I needed the cure, asked,

"Could we skip the lecture and get a pint."

We didn't talk after that. I took my drink and he busied himself on bar stuff. I had got a swig down, a cig lit when the door opened. In marched Michael Tate, carrying a bin liner. He shouted,

"You're on the piss."

"With your huge fee, I just had to celebrate."

He looked like he might attack, said,

"It's true what they say, you're nothing but a rummy."

"There's a word you don't hear much."

Such was his outrage he couldn't quite find the words to articulate it, settled for,

"You're a bloody disgrace."

I decided to try and calm him, said,

"Don't get all bent out of shape, I'll take care of the swans."

"Oh, will you tell me . . ." he lifted the bin liner, "how will you take care of this one?"

Flung it at me.

The bag opened and blood, gore, pieces of swan covered me. I jumped up, going,

"Aw, Jesus."

I could hear Jeff go,

"Hey!"

Tate turned on his heel and walked out. Jeff looked at the mess, said,

"Oh, my God."

I tried for levity, horror bursting my throat, said,

"I'll have to stop bringing work home."

Surgeon Steel.
Deep down inside
A block of ice
Keeps me cool
Keeps me sane
Diamond cut precious death
Hard steel glinting in the
Dark recesses
Splintering glass
Red and blue
Enter my blood stream
And charges towards my
Heart. Surgeon steel
Cutting out the old.

Dolores Duggan

*I met Keegan later in the day. I craved non-judgemental com-*pany. My clothes I had to dump. I was getting through wardrobes like a minor Elton John. Spent an hour in the shower, trying to erase the smell of the blood. A time was, like all Galwegians, I'd regularly feed the swans. It was part of your heritage. Course, like all the best parts of my life, it was long gone. Seemed highly unlikely now I'd ever be able to reenact the habit again. In *Stone Junction* by Jim Dodge, he says,

"I don't know a fucking thing. That must mean I'm finally sane and that's an excellent place to start going crazy again."

Yeah.

Recently opened beside Hidden Valley were Lydl and Argos and, of course, the mandatory luxury apartments. I met my neighbour, wheeling a trolley, crammed with goodies from both stores. I said,

"That'll see you through the winter."

"As long as I don't eat for six months."

He stared over at the new buildings, said,

"I finally figured out the difference between flats and apartments."

Now this I wanted to hear, said,

"Yeah?"

"Sure, if the Corpo give you a place, it's a flat, but if you buy one, it's an apartment."

"Works for me."

"Do you want to hear a joke?"

"Um . . ."

"Guy goes into the library, asks for burger and chips. The assistant says, 'This is the library.' "

I knew the punchline. But in Ireland, never, like never, spoil a story. He was laughing already, in readiness to deliver. I said,

"And?"

"The guy whispers, 'Burger and chips, please.' "

Chances were, he'd get to tell it six more times and be fresh enchanted with each telling. One of the reasons I came home. The English tell jokes with a blend of apology and cruelty. It's not the laughter they enjoy but the derision. Kiki had once asked me about Irish jokes. The English fondness for them and the total lack of English ones in return. I said,

"They laugh at what they're afraid of. We, however, have no fear of them."

She was astonished, asked,

"The English are afraid of the Irish?"

"With good reason."

I'd arranged to meet Keegan in Garavan's, go basic if not ballistic. He was wearing a green wax jacket, Aran sweater and a tweed cap. He asked,

"What do you think?"

"Synge."

"Sing what?"

"The Playboy of the Western World."

"I went to the Aran Islands."

"I'd never have guessed."

"Yo, barkeep, two pints of the black."

He roared this, said,

"They know me in here."

"I don't doubt it."

He whipped off the cap, said,

"Read this."

"The cap?"

"Inside they have a message."

The message read, "Good health to all who wear this."

The pints came and we worked on those. Then he said,

"I learnt a new word."

"And you're going to share?"

"It's *shook*."

"Useful little word."

"Well, Jack, you look shook."

"Thanks."

I told him about the swans. He asked,

"How much was your fee?"

"Twenty quid."

"What! He was paying you per swan?"

"I fucked up, Keegan."

"So . . . put it right."

"I'll try."

He went quiet for a while. A quiet Keegan is a worrying animal. I said,

"Don't go silent on me."

"I have a solution for the gypsy thing."

"Tinker, not gypsy."

"Whatever? Fit him up."

"A frame?"

"Sure. Get some personal stuff from the victims, stash it in his place, he's gone."

I shook my head. He said,

"Come on, Jack, he's garbage, definitely a bad one. Get the scum off the street."

"No, I can't."

"Are you sure you were a cop? OK, I'll do it for you. Your mate, the Sweeper bloke, he'll go along."

"He wouldn't."

"What?"

"He's got integrity."

Keegan was disgusted, said,

"Here's another word I learnt: *bollocks*."

Third drink in, he tells me,

"I'm off."

"Clubbing?"

"No, I mean I'm going back to London."

"When?"

"Tomorrow morning."

"Ah."

"My job's on the line. I'm already a week late."

"Don't go."

"It's all I have, Jack. Without it I'm nothing."

I knew what he meant. All those years later, I clung to my guards persona. The only reality check that would fly, one of the reasons I kept the regulation coat. Like the song, "I, I who have nothing."

He reached in his coat, said,

"You'll need something for the swan gig."

Palmed me an object. I went to look and he said,

"Not here; put it in your pocket."

I did, asked,

"What the hell is it?"

"A stun gun."

"Feels like a cattle prod."

"Same deal with a tad more voltage."

"Aren't they illegal?"

"Course they are, and should be."

I didn't think he'd bought it in Galway, said,

"Surely you didn't bring that through Dublin Airport?"

He drained his glass, gave me a stone look, said,

"You can talk? A bloke who bought coke in."

I was astonished, asked,

"How did you know?"

"I'm a cop, remember? You have a heavy habit going, it stands to reason."

"You never said."

"Hey, that's your affair, crazy as it is. Trust me on this, Jack: that shit will bring you down."

"Thanks for the tip. How does this stun thing work?"

"Point and push."

"Is it effective?"

He gave a demonic laugh; heads turned at the sound. He said,

"Oh, yeah."

Then a thought struck me. I asked,

"Wait a minute, you hadn't planned on giving it to me, had you?"

"No."

"So, Jesus, I mean, you carry it with you as a matter of course?"

"What's your point, Jack?"

"This is Galway. What were you expecting?"

"Your town, boyo, where they behead swans, kill gypsies; you tell me."

I'd no answer so asked,

"What else do you carry?"

He gave a big smile, said,

"Oh, I don't think you want to know, not really."

He was right.

I'd offered to see him off, but he was having none of it, said,

"No, I don't do goodbyes."

The end of the evening, we were standing outside Jury's. I didn't want to let him go. He said,

"You have that look, Jack, like you're going to hug me or something."

"Would I do that?"

"You're Irish, so anything's possible."

I wanted to say "I'll miss you" or something with a bit of weight. I settled for "Take care." He seemed on the verge of emotion, too, but then he aimed a punch, said,

"Stay wired, Jack."

And was gone. I felt a profound sense of loss, turned into Quay Street and began to walk. Four o'clock and the street was hopping. An African combo walloping the bejaysus out of bongos, then a new-ager playing air guitar. He caught my eye. I said,

"Good riff."

"It's for Oasis, man; they're fucked."

I'd gotten as far as Kenny's when two guards approached. I nodded and one said,

"Empty out your pockets."

"What?"

"You're causing a disturbance."

"You're kidding. Look, there's the United Nations of music down there and you're hassling me?"

The second one did a quickstep and they had me pinned. I thought of the stun gun in my pocket and thought,

"I'm screwed."

The first one leant in close, said,

"Superintendent Clancy says you're to watch your step, Jack."

Then he hit me in the kidneys, with a punch I'd delivered myself in my time. It is a bastard. Drops you like a stone; you can't breathe with the pain. As they sauntered off, I wanted to shout,

"Is that your best shot?"

But I couldn't manage the words.

Next morning, I examined the bruise in the mirror. As if a horse had kicked me. It was over a week since I'd done coke and my nerves were raw. Add the hangover to the list and I was but a shout from the mortuary. Heard a parcel come through the door. One of those padded envelopes. My name was typed, so that told me nothing. The postmark was Belfast. Moved over to the table and opened it slowly. Then, holding the bottom, shook it. A hand fell on the table. I staggered back against the sink, bile in my stomach. Tried to focus as my heart riproared against my chest. Looked again, then approached. It was plastic. A note on the palm read,

Need a hand, Jack?

Sweeper arrived at lunchtime, said,

"What happened to you?"

"The guards."

"Now you know what it's like."

He'd bought sandwiches and a thermos of tea. I said,

"There's tea here."

"Tea bags, they're shite."

He laid the sandwiches out, said,

"Rhubarb."

"In sandwiches! It's a joke, right?"

"Try them, you'll be surprised."

"I'd be bloody amazed. No, thanks."

He ate two rounds, wolfed them down. I said,

"Bryson's gone."

"Tell me what he looks like."

I ran down the description. He said,

"We'll find him."

"How?"

"The clans are scattered all over."

"He might be in England."

"More of us there than here."

"What if he didn't do the murders?"

"Why did he run?"

"That's a point."

Sweeper stood, asked,

"How's your English friend?"

"He's gone."

"You keep strange company, Jack Taylor."

If there was a rebuttal to this, I didn't have it. After he left, I tried to read:

"The wind had blown the summer flies away. God had forgotten his own."

This was from Nelson Algren, *The Man with the Golden Arm*.

The phone went.

"Yes,"

"Jack, it's Cathy."

"Hi, Cathy."

"Jeff is gone."

"Gone? Gone where?"

"He's drinking."

"Oh."

"Did you know he hasn't drunk for twenty years?"

"No."

"Will you find him?"

"I will."

"Promise, Jack."

"I promise."

Raymond Chandler in an essay, "The Simple Art of Murder", wrote,

The modern detective is a relatively poor man or he would not be a detective at all. He is a common man or he could not go among common people. He will take no man's money dishonestly and no man's insolence without due and dispassionate revenge. He is a lonely man and his pride is that you will treat him as a proud man or be very sorry you ever saw him. If there were enough like him, the world would be a very safe place to live in, without becoming too dull to be worth living in.

These words were ringing in my ears as I set out to find Jeff. I went to Nestor's. A guy behind the bar I'd never seen before. I asked for Cathy and he said,

"You're Taylor?"

"Yes."

"Go on up, she's expecting you."

She looked terrible, her face wrecked from crying. I gave her a hug, said,

"It will be OK, I'll find him."

"If anything happens to him, Jack . . ."

"It won't. Where would he go?"

"I don't know, I never knew him drinking. At least he didn't take his bike."

The bike was a Harley. Jeff had told me of his two passions, motorbikes and poetry. He'd showed me the bike, said,

"It's a Soft Tail Custom."

I'd nodded sagely as if it meant anything. I sat Cathy down, asked,

"What set him off?"

"People have been sympathising about our damaged baby."

"Jesus."

"I let him down, didn't I, Jack?"

I was no good at this but had to try, said,

"He loves that little girl and you."

"So why did he drink?"

I didn't know, said,

"I don't know."

What I wanted to do was sleep for six months and wake up to good news. Asked,

"Who's the guy behind the bar?"

"From an agency."

"If you're stuck, I could do a turn."

She gave me the look and I said,

"Yea, right, I better get going."

"Tell him I love him."

"He knows that."

"Does he?"

The rain was hammering down. As if it was personal. I tightened my all-weather coat and thought,

"Set a drunk to find a drunk."

Made sense.

Trawled through the likely suspects first. Decided I'd have a drink in every second pub. If I hadn't found him after ten pubs, I'd be beyond caring. Such was a plan, awful as it sounds. In fact, I did five pubs without a drink as nobody should willingly have to endure them. They were bright, noisy, expensive and hostile. I jostled through the crowds of Celtic tiger prosperity. Money had bought a whole new attitude, one of mercenary yahooism. It dawned on me that Jeff wouldn't waste a hot minute in these places. He'd been a musician, so next I hit the series of music venues. Advertising *"Craic agus Ceol"*. Loosely translated, this spells cover charge. To enforce it, the microphone bouncers are on the doors. I said,

"I won't be staying long."

The biggest bouncer grins at his mate, says,

"You got that right."

No Jeff.

I said to myself,

"Think! You were a cop, you're supposed to be an investigator, where would he go? What pub would he have heard of often? Bingo! Yes."

Grogan's, my old stamping ground. I practically lived there when Sean had it. Then he got killed and his asshole son took over. I was no longer welcome. Going in the door was not like going home. It had been renovated. What had been a place full of atmosphere was now just another slice of plastic garbage. Worse, there was musak. That tape which is either Karen Carpenter or the Bay City Rollers or Ronan Keating covering both. Jeff was in a corner. Shot glass and pint on the table. I walked over, said,

"Hey."

"What kept you?"

"I took a wrong turn."

Small smile and,

"Didn't we all."

Sean's son wasn't around so I ordered a pint. Jeff said he'd have a double Paddy. I didn't comment. When I sat down, he asked,

"Got a smoke?"

Course I wanted to say, "You're smoking again," but how redundant was that? Fired him up. He said,

"Wow, this tastes like shit."

"Why do we do it? You don't think we enjoy it, do you?"

He drained the double, took a moment, then,

"Are you going to read me the riot act?"

"Me! I don't think so."

"Good. Did you ever hear of Phil Ochs?"

"Um . . . no."

"A folk singer in the early sixties, he was revered in Greenwich Village, bigger than Dylan. Then he lost it, tumbled into alcoholism. Finished up sleeping in the boiler room of the Chelsea Hotel, where upstairs Leonard Cohen was putting the make on Janis Joplin. Ochs finally hung himself in the bathroom of his sister's house."

I had no idea where this was going so asked,

"And this tells me what exactly?"

"He wrote three great songs, 'An Evening with Salvador Allende', 'Crucifixion' and 'Changes'. Man, those had it all: humour, politics, compassion. Do you know how many great songs I wrote?"

"No."

"None."

We let that circle above our heads, then he said,

"A woman said to me yesterday, nodding at the baby, 'They love music,' as if they were fucking pets."

Jeff never, and I mean *never,* ever cursed. He continued,

"Another one says, 'They bring great blessing to a house'; and my absolute favourite, 'They're all love.' Jesus, I can't get my mind off *Mongoloid.* Is it me or is that an ugly word?

What happens when she gets to school? She'll be bullied, taunted as a retard?"

He stopped, and I said,

"That happens, we'll burn the school."

"They say she won't be able to marry."

"Jeff, buddy, whoa, she's what? Three weeks old and you're worried about marriage? Trust me, marriage isn't so hot."

"I can't handle it, Jack."

"OK."

He stared at me with rage writ large, said,

"I'm serious, Jack. I can't raise a handicapped child."

"So don't."

"What?"

"Raise her the best you can, as Serena May."

"You think?"

"Sure. Don't get lost in the world of mental disability. You don't have to go down that road. You think Cathy and the baby will survive if you're gone?"

He took that, asked,

"What are you planning to do with me?"

"Buy you a drink, then get you home."

"And if I resist?"

"I've got a stun gun."

"You probably do."

The awful thing now was, I wanted to continue drinking. The demons were roaring in my soul, and I thought Jeff would be good company. But I locked down, said,

"If you're ready?"

"Jack, the drinking, how do you keep at it? I'm walloped already."

"Truth is, I don't know."

On the way up Shop Street, he staggered a little but otherwise wasn't too ripped. He said,

"You know she can't be a nun?"

"Serena May?"

"Yea, they don't take Down's syndrome."

"Gee, that's a tragedy, I'm sure you had your heart set on a nun."

"Makes you think, though."

"Jeff, it makes you think they're as black as they're painted."

The Role of the Guards

There are currently around 11,300 guards dedicated to:
1. *The prevention of crime.*
2. *The protection of life and property.*
3. *The preservation of peace.*
4. *The maintenance of public safety.*

I finally took Laura to a dance. As Jack Nicholson said,

"I'd rather have stuck needles in my eyes."

Before going to London, I'd lived in Bailey's Hotel. You have to be old Galway to know it. Well, you have to be old. Off Eyre Square, towards the tourist office, a small street on the left and you're there. The owner was in her eighties, a feisty old devil. A chambermaid, Janet, was even older. She'd once given me a rosary beads. Shortly after, I'd killed my best friend. I'm not saying there's a connection.

It was Janet who told me about the Saturday night dances. Sounded safer than a club and the band was live. If wearing a blazer and being over fifty counts as live. I dressed casual; black jeans, white shirt and a deep anxiety. Arranged to meet Laura in the Great Southern. She asked,

"Why there?"

"So we can begin with notions."

She, as usual, had no idea what I was talking about, but she agreed. As I swung through the revolving doors, the porter said,

"Jack Taylor, by the holy!"

"How you doing?"

I couldn't remember his name so leant heavily on the greeting. Seemed to work as he said,

"Grand. I heard you went to London."

"I'm back."

"That's great, Jack."

I took an armchair in the lobby, just sink in those mothers, feel important.

Laura arrived, short black coat and legs to die for. I clocked the porter give her a look of full appreciation. I stood up and she kissed me, said,

"It's ages since I saw you."

Took her coat off and she'd a black polo over black skirt. I said,

"Jesus, you look phenomenal."

"For you, Jack."

The porter came over, asked,

"Your daughter, Jack?"

"Yes, it's mid-term break."

Laura ordered sherry and I'd a Jameson; get the evening cooking. The porter, trying to regroup, asked,

"Would you be happier in the bar?"

"Nope."

I told Laura about Bailey's. She said,

"Oh, the Saturday dance. My dad used to go."

Whoops!

We'd one more drink and got up to go. The porter took me aside, said,

"Jack, I didn't mean anything by what I said."

"Forget it."

"I wouldn't want to get on the wrong side of the guards."

I didn't correct him. If nothing else, it shows that contrary to popular belief, hotel porters didn't know everything.

Mrs Bailey had a huge welcome, asked,

"Who's this?"

"Laura Nealon."

"Ah, I know all belong to you."

Laura went to the ladies and Mrs Bailey said,

"I heard you got married."

"Not to Laura."

"I thought so. She's far too fond of you to be your wife."

This is Irish flattery at its finest. There's something in there to like, but there's also the suspicion of a lash. Whatever else, it keeps you on your toes. Now she said,

"I wouldn't have you down as a dancer."

"I'm not."

The band didn't disappoint. They had the mandatory blue blazers, white pants. None of them would see fifty again. Not that they'd gone easily into that good night. No, whether it was toupees or Grecian 2000, they'd a uniform of dark unmoving hair. And teeth? Man, they'd molars to die for. Like the showband legacy, they played as if they meant it. The showpiece was the bugles, with a one two dance step to match. Of course, a massive repertoire; if they'd heard it, they played it . . . energetically. From Roy Orbison through the Shadows (with a nod towards the Eagles) to Daniel O'Don-nell. It was *Hospitals' Request* live. The time-honoured for-mula, too: a fast set, ladies choice, then fast. Interspersed was a lone vocalist. The stage would go black, a single spotlight on the singer. He'd stand, head lowered, and a voice would intone,

"Ladies and gentlemen, Elvis Presley" or Chris de Burgh or even Buddy Holly.

Same singer, of course. He had the sort of voice that got no votes on *Opportunity Knocks*. Halfway through the evening, the band took a break; like everybody else, they headed for the bar. As luck would have it, I was alongside the lead vocalist. Sweat was pouring off him. He gasped,

"Howyah?"

"Buy you a drink?"

"No, we got complementaries."

"You deserve it, great show."

"Thanks, it's our last before the tour."

"Tour?"

"Yeah, Canada, then two months in Las Vegas."

I tried not to shudder, said,

"Lucky you."

"And we have an album coming out."

"Wow, what's it called?"

"Greatest Hits."

I had the grace not to ask,

"Whose?"

He lifted a tray of drinks and said,

"There's a chance we'll be on *The Late Late Show.*"

"I'll keep my fingers crossed."

"We'd be made."

"Hey, you're made already."

He loved that. When I tried to pay for my drinks, I was told the band covered it. There are moments, rare as luck, that you feel glad to be alive. That was one. I danced three times, managed to make two of them slow. You can fake your way through these. Just hold her tight and don't walk on her feet, easy-ish. The fast numbers were a nightmare. I tried to look like I had some moves. A woman had once said,

"You learnt to dance in the sixties."

It's one of those statements you don't question. There is never a time you want to hear the answer. Laura, of course, was a great dancer. As I fumbled through, the sweat cascaded down my body, a voice in my head roaring "horse's ass". When we stood for the national anthem, I swore never again. When we walked home, Laura linked my arm and said,

"That was terrific."

Back home, she smiled, went,

"I can stay."

After we'd made love, she perched on one arm, examining me. I wanted to plunge the room into darkness. Her fingers touched the tattoo and she asked,

"Is it an angel?"

"Yes."

"Your guardian angel?"

"I don't know, I got it in a snooker game."

"You won?"

"No, I lost."

One thing my dad had taught me was snooker. He'd played in provincial finals. I'd learnt well. Almost never lost. Till my training at Templemore. We'd a weekend break and had headed for the centre of Dublin. A snooker hall in Mary Street had a long-standing rep. I'd beaten all the other cadets when our sergeant arrived, challenged me to a game. I knew enough then not to play for money, so we'd wager anything else. The sergeant, his sleeves rolled up, was a riot of tattoos. He said,

"You don't approve, young Taylor?"

"Not my thing."

"Well, if you lose, you get one, how would that be?"

Piece of cake, I thought, and lost. Down on the quays we'd gone. Tattoo parlours in those days were dodgy. Of all the awful symbols on offer, the angel was the least offensive. Did it hurt? . . . Like a bastard.

"The fable of one with you in the dark. The fable of one fabling with you in the dark. And how better in the end labour lost and silence. And you as you always were. Alone."

Samuel Beckett, *Company*

I went to the army and navy store and bought heavy-duty polo necks, added thermal leggings and socks. The assistant, a young guy in his twenties, asked,

"How cold are you expecting it to get?"

"Where I'm going . . . very."

"What, like Siberia?"

"No, like the Claddagh."

On my way out, a vaguely familiar face said,

"Howyah?"

I stopped and tried to place him. He had his left ear pierced with four rings. He helped with,

"I used to hang with Cathy in her punk days."

"Oh, right."

"You're the old guy . . . Taylor . . . Yeah?"

"Thanks."

"She said you were a cool dude."

"Thanks again."

I thought he was going to hit me for a loan so I said,

"Good to see you."

"Listen, you want to score some speed?"

On the verge of saying no, I thought, "Hold a mo'." I was pulling an all-nighter, an edge would help. I said,

"Sure, give me a few."

Not cheap. Course the addict in me wanted to drop one immediately, see how it went. My teeth were dancing in their gums from lack of coke. Went home and rang Cathy.

"Jack, how are you?"

"Doing good. How's the man?"

"He's hurting."

"Way it goes."

"But he hasn't taken a cure or anything, so I'm hoping it's finished. Do you think it is?"

"Jeez, Cathy, I don't know. But he has a better shot than most."

"Jack?"

"So you won't try to lure him away?"

"What?"

"Please, Jack?"

"No, I guarantee I won't try to tempt him."

"Thanks, Jack."

Click. I wanted to punch a hole through the wall. The phone went. She was going to apologise. Keegan.

"Are you missing me, boyo?"

"I sure am."

"I did some more checking on Bryson, even spoke to his mother."

"And?"

"Yea, his old man was a vicious drunk and abused the boy in all sorts of ways."

"So he has motivation to hate drunks."

"Yea, . . . but . . ."

"But what?"

"I don't think he's your boy."

"Oh, come on, Keegan, when you were here, you were ready to frame him."

"Listen, Jack, I hate to be wrong. His mother and others say he was always claiming to have done things to get attention. Here's the kicker: he might hate alkies, but he's done an awful lot of good, too, really helped them."

"Sorry, Keegan, the fuck sent me a hand."

"A real one?"

"No, plastic, and trust me, the shock was real enough."

"That's it, Jack. He's a nuisance and needs a kick in the head, that's all."

"Keegan, London has screwed up your head. It's him."

"Look, Jack, there's lots more, I . . ."

"I've got to go, Keegan."

"Jack, come on, think about it."

"I already did. Got to go."

Click.

London was like that, put all sorts of doubts in your head. I'd have to bring Keegan back, straighten him out.

I had hoped never to see Nimmo's Pier again. A daunting task if you live in Galway as it's the crucial point in walking the Prom. That walk is mandatory. I had drowned my best friend from there, with malice aforethought. The largest gathering of swans is at the Claddagh, and the pier is the focal point. There is only one way to approach the birds, and that's down a slipway to the water. Most days, somebody's there, distributing bread. The swans gather at this feeding point. You plan on killing one, this is where you have to do it. A week now since the last slaughter, I got down there at two in the morning. The lights of the city across the bay. I kept my eyes averted from Nimmo's, found a place to hunker down against the wind. In my dark clothes, I was invisible to passers-by. Least, hoped I was.

Clad in my all-weather coat, thermal gear and gloves, I could endure the wind. A black watch cap pulled over my ears. As preparation, I'd filled a thermos with coffee and brandy. Music and laughter floated across the water. I nipped from the flask. My legs were aching with stiffness, and I did some exercises to free them. At four, fatigue came calling and I popped the amphetamines. For twenty minutes, nothing; figured the guy had sold me a dud. Well, I'd have his ass. Next thing, I was near catapulted to my feet with a jolt of energy. Cranked? I was in hyperspace. Into my mind came "Speed kills", followed by "Who gives a toss?" My heart was accelerating by the second, and I was digging it. You're in serious bother when massive palpitations are a buzz.

And buzzing it was. Felt I could bend iron bars with my teeth. The inspiration for a novel came roaring down the pike and I speed-wrote it in jig time. Wanted to shout,

"It's going to be a classic."

Kept hopping up and down like Johnny Rotten at his zenith. Jumped up on the road, begging the swan killer to show. He didn't. Eight o'clock, winding down, I headed home. My face felt raw with twitches, the nerve ends were electric. A milkman said, "Good morning," and I roared, "GOOD MORNING TO YOU." Tried to rein it in but shouted at a postman and a cleaner. Took me two hours to get to the house as my feet propelled me into hundred metre dashes. Finally home, I ran up and down the stairs in a frenzy. With the thermal gear on! The crash when it came was nasty and brutish. Collapsed on the sofa, totally wiped. Focused on the clock and saw it was noon, muttered,

"Not-High Noon."

Slept then till ten at night. Coming round, thought,

"You are no way up to speed."

Tried the restoration stuff: shower, food, coffee, fresh clothes. Barely dented the speed afterburn.

Come midnight, I prepared again. When this was done, I checked the mirror. Not good. The skin on my face was grey, my eyes like high points of lunacy. Trudged again to the Claddagh. Whatever else happened, I wouldn't be using the speed. Took my place against the wall as heavy rain began. If the attacker showed up, the very best I could do was call him names. He didn't show. Odd times, I dozed, just enough to run through a nightmare. Round four, I woke to two swans pecking at my feet. I shouted,

". . . the fuck away!"

They hissed and seemed set to strike. The sound they make is truly intimidating. I forced myself to stay still, and finally they waddled away. I was fast losing my fondness for them. The early hours of the morning, cold wet and depressed, I muttered,

"Am I too old for Tesco?"

The swans were beginning to scare the bejaysus out of me. In the half light, they appeared so menacing. I drank often from the flask, begging the brandy to ignite. As dawn began to break, I swore.

"No more; I'm through with this."

At nine, I moved from my vigil and climbed wearily on to the walk. A spasm of dizziness, and I barely made it to the bench. Tried to light a cig but they were sodden. A short time later, I heard,

"Jack Taylor?"

Turned to see the swan guy. I nodded and he said,

"My God, you look awful."

"It's my disguise."

"Have you been here all night?"

"Yea."

He indicated the houses behind, said,

"Look, I live over there . . . St Jude's. I'll get you breakfast, a hot shower."

"No, I'm OK."

"I apologise for the outburst the other day. I see now you're a conscientious person."

I stood up, said,

"I'll have to go."

He put out his hand, said,

"Thank you for helping."

I'd gotten about a hundred yards when he shouted,

"I'm going to personally see to it that you get another pound."

I was tempted to go,

"My cup overfloweth."

But he was, as the Irish say, "a harmless idiot", so I simply waved my hand. My bile could be better directed.

Laura came by the next evening. She'd bought Chinese and we'd a mini feast. With a shy expression she said,

"I bought wine."

"Great."

"I don't know anything about it."

"Me neither."

Big smile.

"You're a lovely man."

"So, what did you get?"

"Beaujolais, is that all right?"

"Perfect."

Later, she said,

"Something odd happened last night."

"Tell me."

"I went out for a jar with Vicky . . . you know, my friend?"

"Right."

"So, we were in Busker's and these two guys, they kept bothering us, just wouldn't let up. Anyway, when we left, they tried to grab us on the street. Then this man came out of nowhere and . . ." she opened her arms wide, "banged . . ." she brought her palms together, smack, "their heads together, ran them into the wall. He turned to us and said, 'Miss Nealon, you can carry on now.' We were like gobsmacked."

I thought Bill was keeping his word, could only hope when the time came, I'd be able to keep mine. I said,

"Old Galwegians, they look out for each other."

"Oh, it isn't anyone you know?"

"Me? No."

What was I going to tell her, that I'd hired protection. No, I'd keep that deal on the need-to-know basis. There was no way in hell she needed to know. I raised my glass, said,

"*Sláinte.*"

Third night and I'm crouched against the wall. A driving rain found me at every turn. The swans were huddled towards the shore; felt I'd gotten caught in some episode of *The Twilight Zone,* for ever surrounded by unpredictable swans. Had decided to cut out early on this vigil, maybe fuck off home at five. Just after four, a figure stopped at the wall, directly above me. I could hear troubled breathing, like asthma or something. I watched as he approached the slipway . . .

And stepped down.

All I could make out was a long overcoat, wellingtons and, then, a flash of metal. Machete.

He began to walk towards the water. I was up, trying to ease the pain in my joints. I could hear identical sounds to the swans. He was calling them. That spooked me more than anything. Two of the birds were approaching. He raised the knife. I said,

"Yo, shithead."

He turned and I moved nearer. He couldn't have been more than sixteen, blond hair cut short, an ordinary face, nothing to distinguish it, till you saw the eyes. I once read how Hemingway described Wyndham Lewis as having "the eyes of a professional rapist". Here they were. He said,

"Fuck off or I'll cut you."

"Why are you doing this?"

"For me exams."

"What?"

"Lucifer will give me all A's for eighteen heads."

"Eighteen?"

Annoyance crossed his face and he spat,

"Six six six, the number of the beast."

"Jesus."

He ran at me. I let him come, then hit him with the stun gun. The voltage took him off his feet and into the water. I was astonished at the power. As the kid thrashed, it crossed my mind to let him drown. Then the swans went at him. I'd a battle to fend them off as I dragged him out. Took a second to catch my breath and then heaved him over my shoulder. He was groaning as I made my way across the road. I banged on the door of St Jude's till a light came on. Tate opened it and went,

"Oh my God."

"Here's your swan killer."

"What am I supposed to do?"

I laid the kid on the ground, said,

"You better do it quick, whatever it is, as I think the swans took his eye out."

I turned and started to walk. He shouted,

"Where are you going?"

"For a pint."

The story made page one.

LOCAL HERO

Galway born Jack Taylor helped apprehend the person suspected of killing swans. In recent weeks, residents of the Claddagh had been outraged at the attacks.

A spokesperson for the area said, "The swans are part of our heritage."

Mr Taylor, an ex-guard, had mounted a vigil over a number of nights. The alleged perpetrator is believed to be a teenage boy from the Salthill area of the city. Superintendent Clancy, in a brief statement, said:

"The guards are increasingly concerned at the lack of respect by young people for the institutions in the public domain. We will not tolerate wanton vandalism."

He called on parents to play a more active role in the supervision of young adults. Mr Taylor was unavailable for comment.

I'd finally solved a case. Yup, I cracked it. Did I feel good?
Did I fuck. A sense of desolation engulfed me. Cloud of
unknowing? . . . Not quite. I knew and was not consoled.
Emptiness lit my guts like a palpable sense of dread. Back to
basics, back to books. I read as if I meant it. In '91, I came
across David Gates, first novel *Jernigan,* not a book much rati-
fied by addicts. The narrator is boozy, belligerent, demented.
Crucified by his own irony, he is on a course of bended analy-
sis. It depicts the horror of American suburbia. I lent it to a few
people who hated it. I asked,

"What about the humour?"

"You're as sick as Jernigan."

Valid point. Payback though when he was nominated for the
Pulitzer. I settled down to read his short stories titled *Wonders
of the Invisible World*. In "Star Baby", a gay man leaves the big

city for life in his home town, only to find himself cast as a father figure to his detoxing sister's son.

"Mostly he avoids taking Deke to restaurants, not because of the catamite issue but because the two of them look so alone in the world."

I thought what a great word *catamite* was. A little difficult to insert into everyday conversation, but you never knew. The next up was "The Crazy Thought". A woman misses her true love and chafes at city life with an embittered husband.

" 'Nothing wrong with John Le Carré,' Paul said. 'I'd hell of a lot sooner read him than fucking John Updike. If we're talking about Johns here.' "

The doorbell went. I said,

"Shite."

And got up to answer. At first I didn't recognise him, then,

"Superintendent Clancy."

He was in civies, dressed in a three piece suit. A big seller in Penney's three years ago. He asked,

"Might I step in?"

"Got a warrant?"

His face clouded and I said,

"Kidding. Come in."

Brought him into the kitchen, asked,

"Get you something?"

"Tea, tea would be great."

He eased himself into a chair, like someone who has recently hurt his back. He surveyed the room, said,

"Comfortable."

I didn't think it required an answer. I took a good look at him. When I first knew him, he'd been skinny as a toothpick. We'd been close friends. All of that was long ago. His stomach bulged above his pants. Rolls of fat near closed his eyes, his face was scarlet and his breathing was laboured. I put a mug before him, said,

"I'm all out of bickies."

He gave a wolf's smile, said,

"You're to be congratulated."

"On a lack of biscuits?"

Shook his head, said,

"The swan business. You're the talk of the town."

"Lucky was all."

"The other business, the tinkers, are you still pursuing that?"

"No, I got nowhere. Couple of your lads gave me a wallop recently, said you ordered it."

"Ah, Jack, the new lads, they get a touch overzealous."

"So why are you here?"

"Purely social. We go back a long way."

And all of it bad. He stood up, the tea untouched.

"There was one thing."

"Oh yeah?"

"Bill Cassell, our local hard case, you'd do well to steer clear."

"Is that a warning?"

"Jack, you're becoming paranoid. I'm only passing on a friendly word."

"Here's a word for you . . . *catamite*. Look it up, you'll be rewarded."

As he stepped out of the door, a car glided up, a guard got out and opened the rear door. I said,

"Impressive."

"Rank has its privileges."

I gave him the stare, said,

"It shows; you're a man of weight all right."

I'd been reading Derek Raymond again, and noted,

THE CRUST ON ITS UPPERS

It seems to me that no matter whether you marry, settle down or live with a bird or not, certain ones simply have your number on them, like bombs in the war; and even if you don't happen to like them all that much there's nothing you can do about it— unless you're prepared to spend a lifetime arguing fate out of existence, which you could probably do if you tried but I'm not the type.

Over the next few days, I laid low. The most amazing thing had happened. I'd cut back on the booze. The ferocious craving for coke had subsided. Now just a dim ache I could tolerate. Was afraid if I went out, the whole nervous charade would collapse. Read some Merton in a futile search for spiritual nourishment. And got none.

In truth, he now irritated the shit out of me. This usually prefaced a bender of ferocious intent. When Laura rang, I said,

"Hon, I've got flu."

"I'll come mind you."

"No, no, just let me Lim-Sip through it."

"I want to see you, Jack."

"Not sick you don't."

"I don't care."

"Jeez, how many ways do I have to say this, you don't want to see me sick."

"I don't care."

"I do. Three days tops, I'll be fine."

She annoyed me, too. I'd have been hard put to name anything or anyone that didn't. Second day of interment, the doorbell went. Opened it to one of the clan. I'd seen him with Sweeper. I snapped,

"What?"

"Sweeper asked me to check you were OK."

"You checked, goodbye."

Tried to close the door. He put out his hand, said,

"I'm Mikey, could I come in for a minute?"

"A minute, that's it; the clock is ticking."

He came in, glanced round. I asked,

"What were you looking for?"

"Nothing. You've kept the place nice."

He had a studied way of speaking, as if he tasted each word. He asked,

"Any chance of a glass of water?"

I gave him that and he drank deep, said,

"I've a desperate thirst. Must be the rashers I had for breakfast."

"Mikey, why do I get the feeling you have an agenda?"

"I used to live here."

"Sweeper said it was a family."

"No, just me."

"Why did you leave?"

"Sweeper moved me for you."

I lit a red, blew smoke in his direction, said,

"Ah, you're pissed off."

He squeezed the glass, said,

"I wouldn't mind if you'd earned it."

"I found the most likely suspect."

"And he's . . . where?"

I'd had enough, said,

"I've had enough. Was there anything else?"

"No. Could I borrow some books?"

"You read?"

"You think tinkers don't read?"

"Gimme a break. I'm in no mood for persecution gigs."

He didn't move, said,

"So, the books?"

I moved to the front door, said,

"Join the library."

He stood at the step, said,

"You're not letting me have books?"

"Buy your own."

And I slammed the door in his face.

The bell rang again and I pulled it open, ready for fight. It was my neighbour. I said,

"Oh."

He looked rough at the best of times. Now he appeared to have been turned inside out and trampled. He held a bottle, said,

"*Poitín.*"

"Um . . . thanks . . . I think."

"I bought a scratch card, won."

"Much?"

"I've been on the batter for a week."

"That much, eh?"

"I was in a human pub last night."

"A what?"

"You open the door and everybody's singing . . . 'I'm only human'."

I held up the bottle. The liquid was as clear as glass. I said,

"The real McCoy."

He shuddered, said,

"I can vouch for that. The still is in Roscommon."

"I thought the guards were cracking down."

"A guard sold it to me."

"A guarantee in itself."

"None better."

". . . clear to me at last that the dark I have always struggled to keep under is in reality my most unshatterable association . . ."

Samuel Beckett, *Krapp's Last Tape*

Another day of hibernation. On the radio for some reason they're playing an interview with Muhammad Ali. I'm only half listening till,

"The man who views the world at fifty the same as he did at twenty has wasted thirty years of his life."

I'm turning that sucker over.

Jesus.

Figuring it's time to return to crime, bookwise anyway. I get stuck into Lawerence Block; have to speed-read him as Matt Scudder, his hero, speaks at length about recovery from alcoholism. Thin ice at its thinnest. Worse, at one stage, he describes the difference between an alcoholic and a junkie. With the cloud of speed, coke over me and a bottle of *poitín* in the cupboard, I'm between that rock and a hard place. Am I ever? Phew-oh. He writes:

"Show a stone junkie the Garden of Eden and he'll say he wants it dark and cold and miserable. And he wants to be the only one there."

I stood up, got a cig, I was not enjoying this passage. Put on Johnny Duhan's *Flame*. The perfect album for my fragmented state. By the third track, I'm easing down, said,

"OK."

And went back to Block.

"The difference between the drunk and the junkie is the drunk will steal your wallet. So will the junkie, but then he'll help you look for it."

I put the book aside, said,

"Enough, time to go out."

And out I went, more's the Irish pity.

Passing the GBC I thought of my last meeting there with Keegan. On that whim, I went in, got a double cappuccino and an almond croissant. Asked the assistant,

"Don't put sprinkle on."

She was amazed, said,

"How can you drink it without that?"

"With great relish, OK?"

Took a window seat, let the world cruise by. Cut a wedge of the croissant and began to chew. Good? It was heaven. Helped distance the coke craving. A woman approached, said,

"You're Jack Taylor."

Mid bite, I managed,

"Yes."

"Might I have a minute?"

"OK."

She was late fifties but well-preserved. Wearing the sort of suit popularised by Maggie Thatcher. Which told me one thing: "Pay attention." She sat, fixed me with a steady gaze, asked,

"Do you know me?"

"No, no, I don't."

"Mrs Nealon, Laura's mother."

I put out my hand and she gave it a scornful glance, said,

"We're in the same age bracket, wouldn't you say?"

The froth on my coffee was disappearing. I tried for the light touch, said,

"Give or take ten years."

Bad idea. She launched,

"I hardly think Laura's in your range, do you?"

"Mrs Nealon, it isn't a serious thing."

Her eyes flashed.

"How dare you? My daughter is besotted."

"I think you're overstating it."

She stood up, her voice loud.

"Leave her alone, you dirty lecher."

And stormed out.

All eyes in the place on me, high with recrimination. I looked at the pastry, curling in on itself, thought,

"Too sweet really."

The cappuccino had wasted away entirely.

As I slunk out of there, I remembered a line of Borges that Kiki was fond of quoting:

"Waking up, if only morning meant oblivion."

Tried to tell myself the old Galwegian line:

"The GBC is for country people. Them and commercial travellers."

Would it fly? Would it fuck.

Rang Laura, who exclaimed,

"You're better."

"What?"

"Your flu, it's gone."

"Oh, yeah."

"I'm so happy. I bought you a get-well card, it has Snoopy on the front, and I don't even know if you like him. Oh Jack, there's so much I'm dying to know about you. I'll come over right now."

"Laura . . . I . . . um . . . listen . . . I won't be seeing you."

"You mean today?"

"Today and . . . every other day."

"Why, Jack? Did I do something wrong? Did I . . ."

I had to cut this, said,

"I've met someone else."

"Oh God, is she lovely?"

"She's older."

And I hung up.

Lord knows, feeling bad is the skin I've worn almost all my life.
Standing there, the dead phone in my hand, I plunged new depths. Walked to the cupboard, took out the *poitín* and the doorbell went. I said,

"Fuck."

Stomped out and tore the door open. It was Brendan Flood, ex-garda, religious nut, information grand master. Through gritted teeth, I said,

"I gave at the office."

Took him a minute, then,

"I'm not begging."

I moved past him, examined the door. He looked at me questioningly. I said,

"Thought maybe there was a sign here that read 'Assholes Convention'."

Went inside, showed him into the living room. The *poitín*

was neon lit in the kitchen. I gestured to the sofa and he sat. He had a battered briefcase which he placed on his knees. He said,

"You look better, Jack."

"Clean living."

"Our prayers are working, alleluia."

"What do you want?"

He opened the briefcase, began to sort through papers, said,

"You'll know about forensic psychology."

"Not much."

"Despite the guards' lack of interest in the killing of those young men, a forensics man was sufficiently intrigued to make his own study."

"On all the bodies?"

"Yes."

"Why would he do that?"

"He's writing a book."

"And you know him . . . how?"

"He's in our prayer group."

"Of course."

"Here's what he found."

The killer is male, early thirties. A batchelor, only child. Very high IQ. A craftsman. Drives a van that's been refitted. As a child, he'd have killed or tortured animals. Learnt early to cover himself. Growing up, he'd have had minor skirmishes with the law but learn from each mistake. At some stage, he'd have attempted a serious assault on another male. You meet him, he's polite, speaks well, educated but he feels nothing. He's simply not there. Remorse is alien to him. His characteristics are grandiosity and hidden hostility. The psychiatric heading is a narcissistic personality disorder and poor impulse control. Violence is inevitable. Sexual gratification comes with the first kill. He will then be unable to stop.

Flood stopped, asked,

"Could I have a glass of water, please?"

For all the world like Richard Dreyfuss in *Jaws*. I got the water, toyed with the idea of a *poitín* spike, but let it go. As I handed him the water, his hand shook. I said,

"Jeez, this shit really gets to you."

"Please don't swear. Yes, evil deeply disturbs me."

I sat, lit a cig, said,

"Highly impressive, but it amounts to what? I already know who the killer is."

He drank deep of the water, gulped, said,

"Ah, Mr Bryson. That's why I'm here. I'm not sure he fits the profile."

"Profile, bollocks. Where do you think you are? Quantico? Wake up. You're an ex-guard with no future, playing at detection. Believe me, I know how sad it gets. You pray, I drink, and may someone have mercy on our miserable souls."

He was stunned by my outburst. Sat back in the sofa as if I'd hit him. In a sense, I had. A few moments before he spoke, then,

"I didn't realise the depth of your bitterness. I am sorry for your despair."

"Whoa, Flood, back up. I don't want your sorrow."

He took a deep breath, said,

"Jack, these assessments are uncanny in their accuracy."

"So?"

"If it's Bryson, he wouldn't have run."

I stood, said,

"It's him."

He stood, pleaded,

"Jack, listen please. You have that friend, the English police-man, get him to check the background on Bryson, see if it matches the profile."

"Was there anything else?"

"Jack!"

I showed him the door, said,

"Tell your friend I'll buy the book."

"You have a hard heart, Jack Taylor."

"So they tell me."

And I shut the door.

The phone rang continuously that afternoon. I could care. I was the other side of Roscommon's finest.

"In that day you shall begin to possess the solitude you have so long desired. Do not ask me when it will be, or how, in a desert or in a concentration camp. It does not matter. So, do not ask me because I am not going to tell you.
You will not know until you are in it."

Thomas Merton, *The Seven Story Mountain*

There are few nightmares to touch those engendered by poitín.
In the early sixties, there was a classic whine record called "Tell Laura I Love Her". The guy in the song is killed on his motorcycle as he roars the above. I dreamt of this. The guy was Jeff on his Harley, and my Laura is calling my name. I'm covered in swan entrails, and Clancy is coming at me with a machete. I came to in the back yard, rain lashing down upon me. No idea how I got there. The *poitín* bottle was smashed against the rear wall.

I crawled into the hallway and threw up, vomit cascading along my sodden clothes. A thirst burning supreme. Managed to stand and pull the ruined clothes off. Shoved them in the washing machine, turned to max. Then had to force it open, water pouring on to the floor, and ladle in washing powder. Kicked it shut. Into the kitchen and found a can of Heineken, lacerated my fingers attempting to open it. Muttered,

"Thank you, God."

Swallowed half and threw up again. I climbed the stairs and got in the shower. Did five scalding minutes, dried myself slowly as every muscle ached. Nothing kicks the shit out of you as systematically as that *uisce beatha*. No wonder Connemara men drink sherry for penance during Lent. Pulled on jeans and a T-shirt. To my horror, the shirt had a logo. When I finally focused, I read "I'm a gas man."

Fuck.

Lay on the bed and passed out. Didn't wake till late evening. More nightmares. Sat up with a start, my heart pounding. I'd been sick again, so tore the bed linen off. Another shower, feeling one degree less awful. Downstairs to search for another cure. Not a drop: zilch, *nada,* nothing. Had drained everything in the house. I'd have to go out. Last pair of jeans, sweatshirt and my guards coat. Buttoned it tight as a spasm of ice racked my system. A cold from the very dead. The phone went and I nearly didn't answer. If I hadn't, I wonder if things would have turned out any different. Probably not, but I can't help wondering. Picked it up, said,

"Hello?"

"Jack, it's Sweeper."

"Yea?"

"We got him."

"What?"

"In Athlone, working with the homeless."

"Jesus."

"He's asking for you."

"Why?"

"I don't know. Do you want to see him?"

"Um . . . OK."

"I'm sending Mikey for you."

"Tell him I'll be in Nestor's."

"OK."

I headed for the pub. Jeff was behind the bar, looking fit and healthy. The sentry was in place and said,

"Saviour of the swans."

I ignored him. Jeff said,

"You don't look so good, Jack."

"What else is new? You, however, are shining."

"Thanks to you, buddy. I owe you one."

"Yea, yea, gimme a pint and a half one."

For a split second, he hesitated, and I said,

"What?"

He got the drinks. The sentry tried again,

"You're a hero, Jack Taylor."

"Fuck off."

Jeff put the drinks on the counter, said,

"On me."

I got out my money, said,

"No, thanks."

Took the drinks, my hands shaking, and I had to put them back. Jeff was going to help but saw my face and backed off. I took the short in both hands, drained it. The sentry was mesmerised. I said,

"Didn't I just tell you?"

He studied his habitual half empty glass. The whiskey hit my stomach like a rocket. Felt the blood rush to my face, knew I'd have the instant barroom tan. A glow rose from my guts, up through my chest, and I felt the ease. A few seconds later and I could lift the pint with one hand, no tremor. Was about to ask Jeff to hit it again when Mikey appeared at my elbow, asked,

"Bit of a party?"

"You want something?"

"We don't have time. We're having a bit of a party ourselves."

He'd a half smirk. I said,

"Time for a fast one."

I ordered a double and said to Mikey,

"Join me."

"I don't think so."

"Suit yourself."

I lit a cig with the silver Zippo. Mikey said,

"That's Sweeper's lighter."

"So, what's your point?"

He didn't have one. I drained the glass, waited for the jolt, said,

"Let's go."

Jeff said,

"Take care, Jack."

I didn't answer. The Jameson kicked, robbing me temporarily of speech.

Mikey had the van parked outside. Looked battered till you got in and saw it had been custom fit. You could happily live there with all the comforts. I said,

"Nice transformation."

"I'm good with my hands."

He put the van in gear, eased into traffic. I asked,

"Where are we going?"

"Headford Road, the settled community."

The contempt in his voice was like a knife. I didn't bite, and he looked across at me, said,

"I'm not a tinker."

"What?"

"You presume I am."

"Yo, Mikey. I don't presume anything about you. This may be hard to believe, but I don't think about you at all. I met you what . . . once?"

"Twice."

"Twice?

"I was along for the Tiernans, remember? Of course, you just saw a band of tinkers."

I shook my head and got out my cigs, reached for the Zippo. He said,

"I'd prefer if you didn't, not in my van."

I lit up, said,

"Like I give a fuck."

At Woodquay, he said,

"My mother, when I was four, had me out walking at midnight. Ended up at the Fair Green. She tore all her clothes off. Always at a certain point of drink, she'd do that."

When I didn't answer, he continued,

"A van hit her, killed her instantly. Not that she felt anything, she was too drunk for that. The tinkers adopted me."

"Why?"

"Their van."

"What about your family?"

"It was just me and her . . . oh, and the booze. In a flat in Rahoon, remember those? You wouldn't put a dog in them. A Galway ghetto, like America."

I crushed the butt on the floor, said,

"So why'd you stay? You're an adult now."

We were pulling into the driveway of a large house. He said,

"Of all people, you should know there's no going back."

As we got out, I asked,

"Who lives here?"

It was a large three-storey affair with adjoining garage. What it conveyed was cash, lots of it. I couldn't see Mikey's face, but heard the sneer as he said,

"Who else? Sweeper."

"Life is a kind of horror. It is OK, but it is wearing. Enemies and thieves don't lay off as you weaken. The wicked flourish by being ruthless even then. If you are ill, you have to have a good lawyer. When you are handed a death sentence, the newly redrawn battle lines are enclosed. Depending on your circumstances, in some cases you have to back off and lie low. You're weak.
Death feels preferable to daily retreat."

Harold Brodkey, *This Wild Darkness*

Mikey led me into the house. Down a hall lined with black and white photographs. Old Galway. Women in shawls, men in cloth caps. Maybe it was the whiskey, but it appeared a better time. Into a sitting room, lush with antiques and leather furniture. A huge open fire, Sweeper before it, his arm resting on a marble fireplace. Three young men in black tracksuits. Sweeper barked,

"What kept you?"

Directed at Mikey, who glanced at me, said,

"Traffic."

Sweeper turned to me, asked,

"Drink?"

Mikey made a choking sound. I said,

"No, I'm good."

Was I ever? Enveloped in the artificial calm of four whiskies. Sweeper nodded, said,

"I'll take you to him."

Led me through the house. In another room, a woman and three children were watching *Who Wants To Be a Millionaire?* I heard Chris Tarrant ask,

"Final answer?"

We entered the garage. Ronald Bryson was tied to a kitchen chair, naked. A two bar electric fire near him. Sweeper said,

"I'll leave you to it."

A second chair was placed in front of Bryson. His head down on his chest, he appeared to be sleeping. His skin was chalk white, not a single hair on it. I couldn't see any bruising and felt relieved, said,

"Ronald."

His head snapped up, blood around his lips. A moment before he focused, then,

"Dack . . . dank dog."

His teeth were gone, the gums were encrusted with dried blood and spittle. His speech was distorted and barely decipherable. For the sake of sanity, I'll give his words as I finally decoded them. I said,

"You wanted to see me."

He strained against the ropes, said,

"They took my teeth with the pliers."

I wish I'd taken the drink. He said,

"Jack, you've got to tell them it's a terrible mistake. I know I behaved badly but I didn't do those men."

"Yes, you did."

"Jack, please! There's something in me that craves attention. I let people think I did those terrible things but it's . . ."

Then his voce fell into a whisper.

"It's only a game. I do good work, then it's like I'm possessed. I turn against the people I'm helping and start to pretend I've done dangerous stuff. Then I have to move on. You can check. In London . . . loads of times, but it's all fantasy."

I lit a cig, said,

"You trashed my house, made calls, terrorised my girl."

"I only wanted your attention. Have you think I was more than your match."

I stood up and he cried,

"Oh, God, Jack, don't go."

I leant in close to him. Fear rose off his torso like smoke. I said,

"Even if I was to buy any of that, there's one thing that damns you."

"What, Jack? Tell me . . . I can explain . . . anything."

"The hand."

He seemed genuinely confused, asked,

"What hand?"

"One of the victims, his hand was chopped off, left on a doorstep. Then I get a plastic hand in the post. How could you have known about that, unless you did it?"

"Jack, I swear, I don't know anything about hands. I never posted you anything. God Almighty, you have to believe me."

"I don't."

I turned to go and he began to cry, begging me to come

back. I closed the door behind me, went back to the living room. Sweeper asked,

"Did he confess?"

"No."

Sweeper looked into my eyes, asked,

"What's your final word?"

"He did it."

"OK, Mikey will drive you back. I'll call round in a few hours, settle our account."

On the return journey, Mikey didn't speak. I heard a clock strike twelve, thought,

"Call midnight, cry alone."

At Hidden Valley, I was getting out when Mikey said,

"I'm starting to read poetry. Who would you recommend?"

I took a moment as if I was contemplating, said,

"I couldn't give a fuck who you read."

In the house, I was near afraid to keep up the high intensity drinking, decided to attempt to read. Chose Chester Himes; he'd be vicious and funny. From *The Primitive* I underlined the following,

But at this moment of awaking, before her mind had restored its equanimity, phrased its justifications, hardened its antagonisms, erected its rationalisations; at this moment of emotional helpless-

*ness . . . she could not blame it all on the men. That was for cry-
ing, and day for lying; but morning was the time for fear.*

I'd dozed in the armchair. The doorbell went and I got
groggily to my feet. Checked the time. Five o'clock. Sweeper
was alone with a bottle of Black Bush. Led him into the
kitchen. He said,

"I brought cloves, we could have hot ones."

"Why not?"

I boiled the kettle and built big drinks, stirred in the cloves,
sugar, the Bush. Handed him his and sat down. He said,

"It's done."

"OK."

"You want to ask me anything?"

"Would you tell me?"

"Probably not."

We drank and he built the next ones. I said,

"The hand bothers me."

"What?"

"The one in the post."

He gave a short laugh, no humour in it, said,

"That was Mikey."

"What?"

"He goes to Belfast a lot. He thought you needed a wake-up
call. I didn't know till afterwards. The lads told me."

"Oh, my God."

"What?"

"Jesus . . . let me think."

Tried to settle my mind, to recall Brendan Flood's words, said,

"Sweeper, I'm going to describe a person. I want you to listen very carefully and then tell me who comes to mind."

"OK."

I took a deep breath, then began.

"A man in his early thirties, batchelor, high intelligence . . . only child. Good with his hands, drives a custom-fitted van, had a minor run in with the guards, probably gave someone a serious beating once. He's polite, well-spoken, educated."

Sweat was leaking out of me. Sweeper didn't hesitate, said,

"Mikey, why?"

"Nothing, I was curious."

If he'd been less knackered, he might have pushed it. But exhaustion was closing his eyes. He shrugged, took out an envelope, said,

"A bonus. You did well."

"I'm going to move."

"To London?"

"No, back to Bailey's Hotel."

"But you can stay here."

"Thanks, but it's time for a change."

He stood, put out his hand, said,

"I'll be seeing you, Jack Taylor."

"Sure."

After he'd gone, I opened the envelope. Enough to keep me going for a long time. I resealed it.

Next day, I was sitting in Sweeney's. The cries of the seagulls across the docks. Bill Cassell arrived a short time later. He seemed even thinner, took his usual seat, and I sat opposite. I put the envelope on the table, said,

"Will you count that?"

He did, said,

"That's a lot of money, Jack. What do you want? To have somebody killed?"

I lit a cigarette, took a last look at the Zippo, pushed it across to Bill, said,

"His name is . . ."